James Payn

English Lyrics

James Payn

English Lyrics

ISBN/EAN: 9783744766302

Printed in Europe, USA, Canada, Australia, Japan

Cover: Foto ©Andreas Hilbeck / pixelio.de

More available books at **www.hansebooks.com**

ENGLISH LYRICS

.

ENGLISH LYRICS

NEW YORK

D. APPLETON AND COMPANY

1, 3, AND 5 BOND STREET

MDCCCLXXXIV

CONTENTS.

CONTENTS.

vii

CONTENTS.

xii CONTENTS.

CONTENTS. xiii

INTRODUCTION.

THOSE who insist on the original meanings of words may perhaps find it difficult to distinguish between an ode and a lyric, except that the latter term specified the instrument which should accompany the song. But the classes of poem are in fact widely separated, and we feel, if we do not accurately discriminate, the difference between them. It would not be easy to better Mr. Gosse's definition of an ode. 'We take,' he says, 'as an ode any strain of enthusiastic and exalted lyrical verse, directed to a fixed purpose, and dealing progressively with one dignified theme. A lyric, on the other hand, is a short poem dealing with one thought, essentially melodious in rhythm and structure, and, if a metaphor may be taken from the sister art, a simple air, without progression, variation, or accompaniment.

If we wish to make the essentials of a lyric still clearer to ourselves, we shall find we are compelled to do so by negatives. It must not be in blank, nor in heroic verse; save indeed where

2

a refrain, and a subtle repetition of the same words gives lyrical impression, as in Tennyson's 'Tears, idle tears,' and some of the songs in the 'Idylls of the King.' It is not so severe in form as the sonnet; the poet's touch is lighter, even when his subject is grave; a dirge like 'Lycidas' cannot be accounted such, nor a sustained and lofty poem as 'I have led her home' in 'Maud.'

Some of our greatest poets have left no true lyrics, or none into which they have put their best work. Pope's only examples are a burlesque, an imitation of Horace written when he was a mere child, and a paraphrase, also from the Latin; Gray affords us none; no adequately characteristic specimen can be culled from Spenser, or more than one or two from Milton, though the former lived so near in time to Shakspere and Ben Jonson, lyrists if any were, and the latter has been fitly termed 'inventor of harmonies,' so keen was his sense of song.

The present collection, therefore, is in no degree representative of the poets of England in their poetic rank. He who is much here quoted is not necessarily among the greatest, he who has scant or no place may be a far more exalted artist than some who are included, but he has worked less in the special branch of art which now concerns us : a statue of Pheidias could find no room, and if it could would be inappropriate, in a cabinet of gems. Form is always as important in the true lyric, it is sometimes more important than the thought, and just because the verse should be so flawless, it now and then happens that a false note struck in such a poem mars the whole, while it would pass unnoticed in a more sustained work. Thus, no one thinking of ' Lycidas' is in any degree distressed at the line—

> *And oh ye dolphins waft the hapless youth,*

which a modern poet, master of melody, has called ' the only bad line which Milton ever wrote ; ' while

> *Then the might of England flushed*
> *To anticipate the scene,*

is like a fly in ointment, spoiling the whole of Campbell's ' Battle of the Baltic,' though indeed they are not the only blemishes even in that one poem.

The aim is to present in one volume the per- fection of English lyrics, by whomsoever written between the dates selected. Wyatt heads the list, not because there were not a few excellent lyrists earlier than he, but because no earlier poems than his can be written in modern spelling without sacrifice of rhythm and rime, and it is desired that the book should be ' in a tongue understanded of the people.' No living authors are included, and none who have died within the second half of this century. We cannot yet judge them fairly; the living exercise too great a spell over us by their presence; for those but recently gone our tears, as St. Leo said of the Magdalen, have woven a veil which prevents our discriminating what they are who are called up before us.

Odes, properly so called, are excluded; as are all narrative, didactic, and ballad poems. Nor are true lyrics included which will not stand alone. Thus a beautiful song in ' The Lady of the Lake ' finds no place because a line in it is unintelligible apart from the narrative in which it is imbedded. Nor, for the same reason, are extracts given from longer poems.

It is too much to hope that any selection will satisfy all readers, some of whom will no doubt miss favourites, which even if known by heart cannot be read too often :—

As for some dear familiar strain,
Untired we ask and ask again ;
Ever in its melodious store
Finding a spell unheard before :

But the reason for the exclusion of most of these will probably be found in the canons of lyric already laid down.

The Editor's best thanks are due to Mr. E. W. Gosse, Mr. Austin Dobson, and Mr. W. J. Linton, for valuable aid and suggestions.

ENGLISH LYRICS.

SIR THOMAS WYATT,
1503—1542.

THE LOVER PRAISETH THE BEAUTY OF HIS LADY'S HAND.

O GOODLY hand !
　Wherein doth stand
　　My heart distract in pain ;
Dear hand, alas !
In little space
　　My life thou dost restrain.

O fingers slight !
Departed right,
　　So long, so small, so round ;
Goodly begone,
And yet a bone
　　Most cruel in my wound.

With lilies white
And roses bright
　　Doth strain thy colour fair ;

Nature did lend
Each finger's end
    A pearl for to repair.

Consent at last,
Since that thou hast
    My heart in thy demain,
For service true
On me to rue,
    And reach me love again.

And if not so,
There with more woe
    Enforce thyself to strain
This simple heart,
That suffered smart,
    And rid it out of pain.

II.

THE LOVER BESEECHETH HIS MISTRESS NOT TO FORGET HIS STEADFAST FAITH AND TRUE INTENT.

FORGET not yet the tried intent
    Of such a truth as I have meant ;
My great travail so gladly spent,
Forget not yet !

SIR THOMAS WYATT.

Forget not yet when first began
The weary life ye know, since whan
The suit, the service none tell can ;
Forget not yet !

Forget not yet the great assays,
The cruel wrong, the scornful ways,
The painful patience in delays.
Forget not yet !

Forget not ! Oh ! forget not this,
How long ago hath been, and is
The mind that never meant amiss.
Forget not yet !

Forget not then thine own approved,
The which so long hath thee so loved,
Whose steadfast faith yet never moved :
Forget not this !

HENRY HOWARD, EARL OF
SURREY,
III.   1517—1547.

COMPLAINT OF THE ABSENCE OF HER LOVER BEING UPON THE SEA.

O HAPPY dames, that may embrace
    The fruit of your delight,
Help to bewail the woeful case,
    And eke the heavy plight
Of me, that wonted to rejoice
The fortune of my pleasant choice:
Good ladies, help to fill my mourning voice.

In ship, freight with rememberance
    Of thoughts, and pleasures past,
He sails that hath in governance
    My life, while it will last :
With scalding sighs, for lack of gale,
Furthering his hope, that is his sail
Toward me, the swete port of his avail.

Alas ! how oft in dreams I see
    Those eyes, that were my food,

Which sometime so delighted me,
    That yet they do me good.
Wherewith I wake with his return,
Whose absent flame did make me burn.
But when I find the lack, Lord ! how I mourn.

When other lovers in arms across,
    Rejoice their chief delight ;
Drowned in tears to mourn my loss,
    I stand the bitter night,
In my window where I may see,
Before the winds how the clouds flee.
Lo ! what mariner love hath made me.

And in green waves when the salt flood
    Doth rise, by rage of wind ;
A thousand fancies in that mood
    Assail my restless mind.
Alas ! now drencheth my sweet foe,
That with the spoil of my heart did go,
And left me ; but, alas ! why did he so ?

And when the seas wax calm again,
    To chase from me annoy,
My doubtful hope doth cause me plain :
    So dread cuts off my joy.
Thus is my wealth mingled with woe,
And of each thought a doubt doth grow,
Now he comes, will he come ? alas ! no, no.

ENGLISH LYRICS.

6

RICHARD EDWARDS,
IV. 1523—1566.

AMANTIUM IRÆ AMORIS REDINTE-GRATIO EST.

IN going to my naked bed as one that would have slept,
   I heard a wife sing to her child, that long before had
     wept:
She sighed sore and sang full sweet, to bring the babe to
     rest,
That would not cease but cried still, in sucking at her
     breast.
She was full weary of her watch, and grieved with her
     child,
She rocked it and rated it, till that on her it smiled:
Then did she say now have I found this proverb true to
     prove,
The falling out of faithful friends, renewing is of love.

Then took I paper pen and ink, this proverb for to write,
In register for to remain, of such a worthy wight:
As she proceeded thus in song unto her little brat,
Much matter uttered she of weight, in place whereas she
     sat.

And proved plain, there was no beast, nor creature bearing
      life,
Could well be known to live in love, without discord and
      strife:
Then kissed she her little babe, and sware by God above,
The falling out of faithful friends, renewing is of love.

She said that neither king nor prince, nor lord could live
      aright,
Until their puissance they did prove their manhood and
      their might.
When manhood shall be matched so, that fear can take no
      place,
Then weary works make warriors each other to embrace,
And left their force that failed them, which did consume
      the rout,
That might before have lived their time, and nature out:
Then did she sing as one that thought no man could her
      reprove,
The falling out of faithful friends, renewing is of love.

She said she saw no fish nor fowl, nor beast within her
      haunt,
That met a stranger in their kind, but could give it a taunt:
Since flesh might not endure, but rest must wrath succeed,
And force the fight to fall to play, in pasture where they
      feed,

So noble nature can well end the work she hath begun,
And bridle well that will not cease, her tragedy in some :
Thus in song she oft rehearsed, as did her well behove,
The falling out of faithful friends, renewing is of love.

I marvel much pardy quoth she, for to behold the rout,
To see man, woman, boy, beast, to toss the world about :
Some kneel, some crouch, some beck, some cheek, and
    some can smoothly smile,
And some embrace others in arm, and there think many
    awile.
Some stand aloof at cap and knee, some humble and some
    stout,
Yet are they never friends in deed, until they once fall out :
Thus ended she her song, and said before she did remove,
The falling out of faithful friends, renewing is of love.

WILLIAM HUNNIS
died 1568.

V.

THE LOVER CURSETH THE TIME WHEN FIRST HE FELL IN LOVE.

WHEN first mine eyes did view and mark
    Thy beauty fair for to behold,
And when mine ears 'gan first to hark
    The pleasant words that thou me told :
I would as then I had been free
From ears to hear and eyes to see.

And when my hands did handle oft,
    That might thee keep in memory,
And when my feet had gone so soft
    To find and have thy company,
I would each hand a foot had been,
And eke each foot a hand so seen.

And when in mind I did consent
    To follow thus my fancy's will,
And when my heart did first relent
    To taste such bait myself to spill,
I would my heart had been as thine,
Or else thy heart as soft as mine.

Then should not I such cause have found
  To wish this monstrous sight to see,
Nor thou, alas ! that madest the wound,
  Should not deny me remedy :
Then should one will in both remain,
To ground one heart which now is twain.

GEORGE GASCOIGNE,
VI.　　　　　　　　　　1535?—1577.

THE LULLABY OF A LOVER.

SING lullaby, as women do,
　Wherewith they bring their babes to rest ;
And lullaby can I sing too,
　As womanly as can the best.
With lullaby they still the child ;
And, if I be not much beguiled,
Full many a wanton babe have I,
Which must be stilled with lullaby.

First lullaby my youthful years,
　It is now time to go to bed :
For crooked age and hoary hairs
　Have won the haven within my head.
With lullaby then youth be still ;
With lullaby content thy will ;
Since courage quails and comes behind,
Go sleep and so beguile thy mind !

3

Next, lullaby my gazing eyes,
　　Which wonted were to glance apace ;
For every glass may now suffice
　　To show the furrows in my face.
With lullaby then wink awhile ;
With lullaby your looks beguile ;
Let no fair face, nor beauty bright,
Entice you eft with vain delight.

And lullaby my wanton will ;
　　Let reason's rule now rein thy thought ;
Since all too late I find by skill
　　How dear I have thy fancies bought ;
With lullaby now take thine ease,
With lullaby thy doubts appease ;
For trust to this, if thou be still,
My body shall obey thy will.

Eke lullaby my loving boy,
　　My little robin take thy rest ;
Since age is cold and nothing coy,
　　Keep close thy coin, for so is best.
With lullaby be thou content ;
With lullaby thy lusts relent.
Let others pay which have more pence ;
Thou art too poor for such expense.

Thus lullaby my youth, mine eyes,
  My will, my ware, and all that was:
I can no more delays devise ;
  But welcome pain, let pleasure pass.
With lullaby now take your leave,
With lullaby your dreams deceive,
And when you rise with waking eye,
Remember then this lullaby.

NICHOLAS BRETON,
1542—1626?

VII.

A PASTORAL OF PHILLIS AND CORYDON.

O N a hill there grows a flower,
   Fair befall the dainty sweet ;
By that flower there is a bower,
   Where the heavenly Muses meet.

In that bower there is a chair,
   Fringed all about with gold ; .
Where doth sit the fairest fair
   That ever eye did yet behold.

It is Phillis fair and bright,
   She that is the shepherd's joy ;
She that Venus did despite,
   And did blind her little boy.

This is she, the wise, the rich,
   That the world desires to see ;
This is *ipsa quæ* the which,
   There is none but only she.

Who would not this face admire?
   Who would not this saint adore?
Who would not this sight desire,
   Though he thought to see no more?

Oh fair eyes, yet let me see,
   One good look, and I am gone;
Look on me, for I am he,
   Thy poor silly Corydon.

Thou that art the shepherd's queen,
   Look upon thy silly swain;
By thy comfort have been seen
   Dead men brought to life again.

VIII.

CORYDON'S SUPPLICATION TO PHILLIS.

SWEET Phillis, if a silly swain,
   May sue to thee for grace;
See not thy loving shepherd slain,
   With looking on thy face.
But think what power thou hast got,
   Upon my flock and me;
Thou seest they now regard me not,
   But all do follow thee.

And if I have so far presum'd,
  With prying in thine eyes;
Yet let not comfort be consum'd,
  That in thy pity lies.
But as thou art that Phillis fair,
  That Fortune favour gives;
So let not Love die in despair,
  That in thy favour lives.
The deer do browse upon the brier,
  The birds do pick the cherries;
And will not Beauty grant Desire
  One handful of her berries?
If it be so that thou hast sworn
  That none shall look on thee;
Yet let me know thou dost not scorn
  To cast a look on me.
But if thy beauty make thee proud,
  Think then what is ordain'd;
The heavens have never yet allow'd
  That Love should be disdain'd.
Then lest the fates that favour Love,
  Should curse thee for unkind;
Let me report for thy behoof,
  The honour of thy mind;
Let Corydon with full consent,
  Set down what he hath seen;
That Phillida with Love's content,
  Is sworn the Shepherd's Queen.

IX.

OLDEN LOVE-MAKING.

IN time of yore when shepherds dwelt
    Upon the mountain rocks ;
And simple people never felt
    The pain of lovers' mocks ;
But little birds would carry tales
    'Twixt Susan and her sweeting ;
And all the dainty nightingales
    Did sing at lovers' meeting ;
Then might you see what looks did pass
    Where shepherds did assemble ;
And where the life of true love was,
    When hearts could not dissemble.

Then yea and nay was thought an oath
    That was not to be doubted ;
And when it came to faith and troth
    We were not to be flouted.
Then did they talk of curds and cream,
    Of butter, cheese, and milk ;
There was no speech of sunny beam
    Nor of the golden silk.

Then for a gift a row of pins,
　　A purse, a pair of knives ;
Was all the way that love begins,
　　And so the shepherd wives.

But now we have so much ado,
　　And are so sore aggrieved ;
That when we go about to woo
　　We cannot be believed.
Such choice of jewels, rings and chains
　　That may but favour move ;
And such intolerable pains
　　Ere one can hit on love.
That if I still shall bide this life
　　'Twixt love and deadly hate ;
I will go learn the country life,
　　Or leave the lover's state.

EDWARD VERE, EARL OF
OXFORD,
1545—1604.

THE BIRTH OF DESIRE.

COME hither, shepherd swain !
   Sir, what do you require ?
I pray thee shew to me thy name !
   My name is fond Desire.

When wert thou born, Desire ?
   In pomp and prime of May.
By whom, sweet boy, wert thou begot ?
   By fond Conceit, men say.

Tell me, who was thy nurse ?
   Fresh youth in sugared joy.
What was thy meat and daily food ?
   Sad sighs, with great annoy.

What hadst thou then to drink ?
   Unsavoury lovers' tears.
What cradle wert thou rocked in ?
   In hope devoid of fears.

What lulled thee then asleep?
  Sweet speech, which likes me best.
Tell me where is thy dwelling place?
  In gentle hearts I rest.

What thing doth please thee most?
  To gaze on beauty still.
Whom dost thou think to be thy foe?
  Disdain of my good will.

Doth company displease?
  Yes, surely, many one.
Where doth Desire delight to live?
  He loves to live alone.

Doth either time or age
  Bring him unto decay?
No! no, Desire both lives and dies
  A thousand times a day.

Then fond Desire, farewell,
  Thou art not mate for me,
I should be loth methinks to dwell
  With such a one as thee.

SIR EDWARD DYER,
1550?—1607.

XI.

MY MIND TO ME A KINGDOM IS.

MY mind to me a kingdom is,
    Such present joys therein I find,
That it excels all other bliss
    That earth affords or grows by kind:
Though much I want which most would have,
Yet still my mind forbids to crave.

No princely pomp, no wealthy store,
    No force to win the victory,
No wily wit to salve a sore,
    No shape to feed a loving eye;
To none of these I yield as thrall:
For why? my mind doth serve for all.

I see how plenty surfeits oft,
    And hasty climbers soon do fall;
I see that those which are aloft
    Mishap doth threaten most of all;
They get with toil, they keep with fear:
Such cares my mind could never bear.

Content I live, this is my stay,
   I seek no more than may suffice ;
I press to bear no haughty sway ;
   Look what I lack my mind supplies:
Lo thus I triumph like a king,
Content with that my mind doth bring.

Some have too much, yet still do crave ;
   I little have, and seek no more.
They are but poor though much they have,
   And I am rich with little store ;
They poor, I rich ; they beg, I give ;
They lack, I leave ; they pine, I live.

I laugh not at another's loss,
   I grudge not at another's gain ;
No worldly waves my mind can toss ;
   My state at one doth still remain :
I fear no foe, I fawn no friend ;
I loathe not life, nor dread my end.

Some weigh their pleasure by their lust,
   Their wisdom by their rage of will ;
Their treasure is their only trust,
   A cloked craft their store of skill.
But all the pleasure that I find
Is to maintain a quiet mind.

My wealth is health and perfect ease,
   My conscience clear my choice defence ;
I neither seek by bribes to please,
   Nor by deceit to breed offence :
Thus do I live, thus will I die ;
Would all did so well as I.

Sir Walter Raleigh,
1552—1618.

XII.

THE SHEPHERD TO THE FLOWERS.

SWEET violets, Love's paradise, that spread
   Your gracious odours, which you couched bear
     Within your paly faces;
Upon the gentle wing of some calm-breathing wind
     That plays amidst the plain,
     If by the favour of propitious stars you gain
Such grace as in my lady's bosom place to find;
     Be proud to touch those places.
And when her warmth your moisture forth doth wear,
Whereby her dainty parts are sweetly fed;
     Your honours of the flowery meads I pray,
      You pretty daughters of the earth and sun;
     With mild and seemly breathing straight display
      My bitter sighs, that have my heart undone.

Vermilion roses, that with new day's rise
Display your crimson folds fresh-looking fair,
     Whose radiant bright disgraces
The rich adorned rays of roseate rising morn;

Ah ! if her virgin's hand
Do pluck your pure, ere Phœbus view the land,
And vail your gracious pomp in lovely Nature's scorn.
If chance my mistress traces
Fast by your flowers to take the summer's air ;
Then woeful blushing tempt her glorious eyes,
To spread their tears, Adonis' death reporting,
And tell Love's torments, sorrowing for her friend ;
Whose drops of blood within your leaves consorting,
Report fair Venus' moans to have no end.
Then may Remorse in pitying of my smart,
Dry up my tears, and dwell within her heart.

XIII.

DISPRAISE OF LOVE, AND LOVERS' FOLLIES.

IF love be life, I long to die,
   Live they that list for me :
And he that gains the most thereby,
   A fool at least shall be.
But he that feels the sorest fits,
'Scapes with no less than loss of wits.
   Unhappy life they gain,
   Which love do entertain.

In day by feigned looks they live,
　By lying dreams in night ;
Each frown a deadly wound doth give,
　Each smile a false delight.
If 't hap their lady pleasant seem,
It is for others' love they deem :
　　If void she seem of joy,
　　Disdain doth make her coy.

Such is the peace that lovers find,
　Such is the life they lead,
Blown here and there with every wind,
　Like flowers in the mead.
Now war, now peace, now war again,
Desire, despair, delight, disdain,
　　Though dead in midst of life,
　　In peace and yet at strife.

XIV.

SIR PHILIP SIDNEY,
1554—1586.

A DITTY.

M Y true love hath my heart, and I have his,
    By just exchange one to the other given :
I hold his dear, and mine he cannot miss,
    There never was a better bargain driven :
        My true love hath my heart, and I have his.

His heart in me keeps him and me in one,
    My heart in him his thoughts and senses guides :
He loves my heart, for once it was his own,
    I cherish his because in me it abides.
        My true love hath my heart, and I have his.

XV.

ASTROPHEL'S LOVE IS DEAD.

R ING out your bells, let mourning shews be spread,
        For Love is dead.
    All love is dead infected
        With plague of deep disdain :

4

Worth as nought worth rejected,
   And faith fair scorn doth gain.
From so ungrateful fancy,
From such a female frenzy,
From them that use men thus:
   Good Lord deliver us.

Weep neighbours weep, do you not hear it said
   That Love is dead?
   His death-bed peacocks folly,
     His winding-sheet is shame:
   His will false, seeming holy,
     His sole executor blame.
From so ungrateful fancy,
From such a female frenzy,
From them that use me thus:
   Good Lord deliver us.

Let dirge be sung, and trentals richly read,
   For Love is dead.
   And wrong his tomb ordaineth,
     My mistress' marble heart:
   Which epitaph containeth,
     Her eyes were once his dart.
From so ungrateful fancy,
From such a female frenzy,
From them that use men thus:
   Good Lord deliver us.

Alas ! I lie, rage hath this error bred,
   Love is not dead.
Love is not dead, but sleepeth
   In her unmatched mind :
Where she his counsel keepeth,
   Till due desert she find.
Therefore from so vile fancy,
To call such wit a frenzy,
Who love can temper thus :
   Good Lord deliver us.

HENRY CONSTABLE,
1555?—1615?

XVI.

DAMELUS' SONG TO HIS DIAPHENIA.

DIAPHENIA like the daffadowndilly,
   White as the sun, fair as the lily,
  Heigh-ho, how I do love thee !
I do love thee as my lambs
Are beloved of their dams,
   How blest were I if thou would'st prove me !

Diaphenia like the spreading roses,
That in thy sweets all sweets incloses,
   Fair sweet how I do love thee !
I do love thee as each flower
Loves the sun's life-giving power.
    For dead, thy breath to life might move me.

Diaphenia like to all things blessed,
When all thy praises are expressed,
   Dear joy, how I do love thee !
As the birds do love the spring,
Or the bees their careful king ;
   Then in requite, sweet virgin, love me.

THOMAS LODGE,
1557?—1625?

XVII.

MADRIGAL.

THE earth late choked with showers
   Is now arrayed in green ;
Her bosom springs with flowers,
   The air dissolves her teen,
The heavens laugh at her glory :
Yet bide I sad and sorry.

The woods are decked with leaves,
   And trees are clothed gay,
And Flora crowned with sheaves
   With oaken boughs doth play :
Where I am clad in black,
The token of my wrack.

The birds upon the trees
   Do sing with pleasant voices,
And chant in their degrees
   Their loves and lucky choices :
When I whilst they are singing,
With sighs mine arms am wringing.

The thrushes seek the shade,
    And I my fatal grave ;
Their flight to heaven is made,
    My walk on earth I have :
They free, I thrall : they jolly,
I sad and pensive wholly.

XVIII.

ROSALIND'S MADRIGAL.

L OVE in my bosom, like a bee,
        Doth suck his sweet ;
Now with his wings he plays with me,
        Now with his feet.
Within mine eyes he makes his nest,
His bed amidst my tender breast ;
My kisses are his daily feast,
And yet he robs me of my rest.
        Ah ! wanton, will ye ?

And if I sleep, then percheth he
        With pretty flight,
And makes his pillow of my knee,
        The livelong night.

Strike I my lute, he tunes the string ;
He music plays if so I sing ;
He lends me every lovely thing :
Yet cruel he my heart doth sting :
  Whist, wanton, still ye.

Else I with roses every day
  Will whip you hence,
And bind you when you long to play,
  For your offence.
I'll shut mine eyes to keep you in,
I'll make you fast it for your sin,
I'll count your power not worth a pin.
Alas ! what hereby shall I win
  If he gainsay me ?

What if I beat the wanton boy
  With many a rod ?
He will repay me with annoy,
  Because a god.
Then sit thou safely on my knee,
And let thy bower my bosom be ;
Lurk in mine eyes, I like of thee :
O Cupid ! so thou pity me,
  Spare not but play thee.

XIX.

MONTANUS' FANCY.

GRAVEN UPON THE BARK OF A TALL BEECH TREE.

FIRST shall the heavens want starry light,
  The seas be robbed of their waves;
The day want sun, and sun want bright,
  The night want shade, the dead men graves.
The April, flowers and leaf and tree,
Before I false my faith to thee.

First shall the tops of highest hills
  By humble plains be overpride:
And poets scorn the Muses' quills,
  And fish forsake the water glide;
And Iris loose her coloured weed,
Before I fail thee at thy need.

First direful hate shall turn to peace,
  And love relent in deep disdain;
And death his fatal stroke shall cease,
  And envy pity every pain,
And pleasure mourn, and sorrow smile,
Before I talk of any guile.

First time shall stay his stayless race,
   And winter bless his brows with corn:
And snow bemoisten Julia's face,
   And winter, spring, and summer mourn,
Before my pen by help of fame,
Cease to recite thy sacred name.

XX.

MONTANUS' PRAISE OF HIS FAIR PHŒBE.

PHŒBE sat,
   Sweet she sat,
  Sweet sat Phœbe when I saw her;
White her brow,
Coy her eye,
  Brow and eye, how much you please me!
Words I spent,
Sighs I sent,
  Sighs and words could never draw her.
Oh my love,
Thou art lost,
  Since no sight could ever ease thee.
Phœbe sat
By a fount,
  Sitting by a fount I spied her:

Sweet her touch,
Rare her voice ;
   Touch and voice, what may distain you?
As she sung,
I did sigh,
   And by sighs whilst that I tried her,
Oh mine eyes,
You did lose
   Her first sight whose want did pain you.
Phœbe's flocks
White as wool,
   Yet were Phœbe's locks more whiter.
Phœbe's eyes,
   Dove-like mild,
   Dove-like eyes both mild and cruel.
Montan swears
In your lamps
   He will die for to delight her.
Phœbe yield,
Or I die :
   Shall true hearts be fancy's fuel?

XXI.

VIRELAY.

ACCURST be love, and they that trust his trains;
He tastes the fruit, whil'st others toil:
He brings the lamp, we lend the oil:
He sows distress, we yield him soil:
He wageth war, we bide the foil.

Accurst be love, and those that trust his trains:
He lays the trap, we seek the snare:
He threatneth death, we speak him fair:
He coins deceits, we foster care:
He favoureth pride, we count it rare.

Accurst be love, and those that trust his trains;
He seemeth blind, yet wounds with art:
He vows content, he pays with smart:
He swears relief, yet kills the heart:
He calls for truth, yet scorns desert.
Accurst be love, and those that trust his trains.
Whose heaven is hell; whose perfect joys are pains.

ROBERT GREENE,
XXII.   1560?—1592.

DORON'S DESCRIPTION OF HIS FAIR SHEPHERDESS SAMELA.

L IKE to Diana in her summer weed,
 Girt with a crimson robe of brightest dye,
   Goes fair Samela.
Whiter than be the flocks that straggling feed,
When washed by Arethusa fount they lie,
   Is fair Samela.
As fair Aurora in her morning gray,
Decked with the ruddy glister of her love ;
   Is fair Samela.
Like lovely Thetis on a calmed day,
Whenas her brightness Neptune's fancies move ;
   Shines fair Samela.
Her tresses gold, her eyes like glassy streams,
Her teeth are pearl, the breasts are ivory,
   Of fair Samela.
Her cheeks, like rose and lily, yield forth gleams,
Her brows bright arches framed of ebony,
   Thus fair Samela

Passeth fair Venus in her bravest hue,
And Juno in the show of majesty,
      For she's Samela.
Pallas in wit, all three you well may view,   .
For beauty, wit, and matchless dignity,
      Yield to Samela.

XXIII.

SONG.

AH ! were she pitiful as she is fair,
 Or but as mild as she is seeming so,
Then were my hopes greater than my despair,
 Then all the world were heaven, nothing woe.
Ah ! were her heart relenting as her hand,
 That seems to melt even with the mildest touch,
Then knew I where to seat me in a land,
 Under wide heavens, but yet there is not such.
So as she shows, she seems the budding rose,
 Yet sweeter far than is an earthly flower,
Sovereign of beauty, like the spray she grows ;
 Compassed she is with thorns and cankered bower,
Yet were she willing to be plucked and worn,
She would be gathered, though she grew on thorn.

Ah ! when she sings, all music else be still,
   For none must be compared to her note ;
Ne'er breathed such glee from Philomela's bill,
   Nor from the morning-singer's swelling throat.
Ah ! when she riseth from her blissful bed,
   She comforts all the world as doth the sun,
And at her sight the night's foul vapour's fled ;
   When she is set, the gladsome day is done.
O glorious sun ! imagine me the west,
Shine in my arms, and set thou in my breast.

ROBERT SOUTHWELL,
1560—1595.

XXIV.

THE BURNING BABE.

AS I in hoary winter's night
   Stood shivering in the snow,
Surprised I was with sudden heat,
   Which made my heart to glow ;
And lifting up a fearful eye
   To view what fire was near,
A pretty babe all burning bright,
   Did in the air appear ;
Who scorched with excessive heat,
   Such floods of tears did shed,
As though his floods should quench his flames,
   Which with his tears were bred.
'Alas !' quoth he, 'but newly born,
   In fiery heats I fry,
Yet none approach to warm their hearts
   Or feel my fire, but I ;

My faultless breast the furnace is,
   The fuel, wounding thorns ;
Love is the fire, and sighs the smoke,
   The ashes, shames and scorns ;

The fuel justice layeth on,
  And mercy blows the coals,
The metal in this furnace wrought
  Are men's defiled souls :
For which, as now on fire I am,
  To work them to their good,
So will I melt into a bath,
  To wash them in my blood !
With this he vanished out of sight,
  And swiftly shrunk away,
And straight I called unto my mind
  That it was Christmas Day.

SIR FRANCIS BACON,
1561—1626.

XXV.

LIFE.

THE World's a bubble ; and the life of man
    Less than a span :
In his conception wretched ; from the womb,
    So to the tomb :
Curst from the cradle, and brought up to years,
    With cares and fears.
Who then to frail Mortality shall trust
But limmes the water, or but writes in dust.

Yet, since with sorrow here we live opprest,
    What life is best ?
Courts are but only superficial schools
    To dandle fools :
The rural parts are turned into a den
    Of savage men :
And where's a city from all vice so free
But may be termed the worst of all the three ?

Domestic cares afflict the husband's bed,
    Or pains, his head :

5

Those that live single, take it for a curse,
　　　　Or do things worse :
Some would have children ; those that have them none ;
　　　　Or wish them gone.
What is it then to have or have no wife
But single thraldom or a double strife ?

Our own affections still at home to please,
　　　　Is a disease :
To cross the sea to any foreign soil,
　　　　Perils and toil :
Wars with their noise affright us : when they cease
　　　　We are worse in peace.
What then remains, but that we still should cry,
Not to be born, or being born, to die.

SAMUEL DANIEL,
1562—1619.

XXVI.

SONG.

L OVE is a sickness full of woes,
    All remedies refusing ;
A plant that with most cutting grows,
    Most barren with best using
      Why so ?
More we enjoy it, more it dies ;
If not enjoyed, it sighing cries,
      Hey, ho !

Love is a torment of the mind,
    A tempest everlasting ;
And Jove hath made it of a kind
    Not well, nor full, nor fasting.
      Why so ?
More we enjoy it, more it dies ;
If not enjoyed, it sighing cries,
      Hey, ho !

XXVII.

ULYSSES AND THE SIREN.

SIREN.

COME worthy Greek, Ulysses, come,
　　Possess these shores with me,
The winds and seas are troublesome,
　　And here we may be free.
Here may we sit and view their toil
　　That travail in the deep,
And joy the day in mirth the while,
　　And spend the night in sleep.

ULYSSES.

Fair nymph, if fame or honour were
　　To be attained with ease,
Then would I come and rest with thee,
　　And leave such toils as these.
But here it dwells, and here must I
　　With danger seek it forth,
To spend the time luxuriously
　　Becomes not men of worth.

SIREN.

Ulysses, O be not deceived
　　With that unreal name,

'Tis honour is a thing conceived,
  And rests on others fame.
Begotten only to molest
  Our peace, and to beguile,
The best thing of our life, our rest,
  And give us up to toil.

ULYSSES.

Delicious nymph, suppose there were
  Nor honour nor report,
Yet manliness would scorn to wear
  The time in idle sport ;
For toil doth give a better touch
  To make us feel our joy,
And ease finds tediousness as much
  As labour yields annoy.

SIREN.

Then pleasure likewise seems the shore
  Whereto tends all your toil,
Which you forego to make it more,
  And perish oft the while.
Who may disport them diversely
  Find never tedious day,
And ease may have variety
  As well as action may.

ULYSSES.

But natures of the noblest frame
  These toils and dangers please,
And they take comfort in the same
  As much as you in ease ;
And with the thought of actions past
  Are recreated still :
When pleasure leaves a touch at last
  To show that it was ill.

SIREN.

That doth opinion only cause,
  That's out of custom bred,
Which makes us many other laws
  Than ever nature did.
No widows wail for our delights,
  Our sports are without blood,
The world we see by warlike wights
  Receives more hurt than good.

ULYSSES.

But yet the state of things require
  These motions of unrest :
And these great spirits of high desire
  Seem born to turn them best.
To purge the mischiefs that increase,
  And all good order mar,

For oft we see a wicked peace
To be well changed for war.

SIREN.

Well, well, Ulysses, then I see,
I shall not have thee here:
And therefore I will come to thee,
And take my fortune there.
I must be won that cannot win,
Yet lost were I not won,
For beauty hath created been
To undo, or be undone.

XXVIII.

CHRISTOPHER MARLOWE,
1564—1593.

SONG.

COME live with me and be my love,
And we will all the pleasures prove,
That grove or valley, hill or field,
Or wood and steepy mountain yield.

Where we will sit on rising rocks,
And see the shepherds feed their flocks
By shallow rivers, to whose falls
Melodious birds sing madrigals.

Pleased will I make thee beds of roses,
And twine a thousand fragrant posies ;
A cap of flowers, and rural kirtle,
Embroidered all with leaves of myrtle.

A jaunty gown of finest wool,
Which from our pretty lambs we pull ;
And shoes lined choicely for the cold,
With buckles of the purest gold.

A belt of straw, and ivy buds,
With coral clasps, and amber studs ;
If these, these pleasures can thee move,
To live with me, and be my love.

XXIX. ANON.

THE SHEPHERD'S SONG.

WHILE that the sun with his beams hot
  Scorched the fruits in vale and mountain,
Philon the shepherd, late forgot,
  Sitting beside a crystal fountain,
    In shadow of a green oak tree
    Upon his pipe this song played he :
Adieu Love, adieu Love, untrue Love,
Untrue Love, untrue Love, adieu Love ;
Your mind is light, soon lost for new love.

So long as I was in your sight
  I was your heart, your soul, and treasure ;
And evermore you sobbed and sighed
  Burning in flames beyond all measure :
    Three days endured your love to me,
    And it was lost in other three !
Adieu Love, adieu Love, untrue Love,
Untrue Love, untrue Love, adieu Love ;
Your mind is light, soon lost for new love.

Another shepherd you did see
  To whom your heart was soon enchained ;

Full soon your love was leapt from me,
　Full soon my place he had obtained.
　　Soon came a third, your love to win,
　　And we were out and he was in.
Adieu Love, adieu Love, untrue Love,
Untrue Love, untrue Love, adieu Love ;
Your mind is light, soon lost for new love.

Sure you have made me passing glad
　That you your mind so soon removed,
Before that I the leisure had
　To choose you for my best beloved :
　　For all your love was past and done
　　Two days before it was begun :—
Adieu Love, adieu Love, untrue Love,
Untrue Love, untrue Love, adieu Love ;
Your mind is light, soon lost for new love.

WILLIAM SHAKSPERE,
1564—1616.

XXX.

BALTHAZAR'S SONG.

SIGH no more, ladies, sigh no more,
    Men were deceivers ever,
One foot in sea, and one on shore,
    To one thing constant never.
        Then sigh not so,
        But let them go,
    And be you blithe and bonny,
Converting all your sounds of woe
    Into Hey nonny, nonny.

Sing no more ditties, sing no mo,
    Of dumps so dull and heavy ;
The fraud of men was ever so,
    Since summer first was leavy.
        Then sigh not so,
        But let them go,
    And be you blithe and bonny,
Converting all your sounds of woe
    Into Hey nonny, nonny.

XXXI.

FAIRIES' SONG.

YOU spotted snakes with double tongue,
    Thorny hedge-hogs, be not seen ;
Newts, and blind-worms, do no wrong ;
    Come not near our fairy queen.
    Philomel, with melody
    Sing in our sweet lullaby ;
Lulla, lulla, lullaby ; lulla, lulla, lullaby :
      Never harm,
      Nor spell nor charm,
    Come our lovely lady nigh ;
    So, good night, with lullaby.

Weaving spiders, come not here ;
    Hence, you long-legged spinners, hence !
Beetles black, approach not near ;
    Worm nor snail, do no offence.
    Philomel, with melody
    Sing in our sweet lullaby ;
Lulla, lulla, lullaby ; lulla, lulla, lullaby :
      Never harm,
      Nor spell nor charm,
    Come our lovely lady nigh ;
    So, good night, with lullaby.

XXXII.

SONG.

TELL me where is fancy bred,
　　Or in the heart or in the head?
How begot, how nourished?
　　Reply, reply.
It is engendered in the eyes,
With gazing fed; and fancy dies
In the cradle where it lies.
　　Let us all ring fancy's knell:
　　I'll begin it,—Ding, dong, bell.
Ding dong, bell.

XXXIII.

ARIEL'S SONG.

WHERE the bee sucks, there suck I:
　　In a cowslip's bell I lie;
There I couch when owls do cry.
On the bat's back I do fly
After summer merrily.
Merrily, merrily shall I live now
Under the blossom that hangs on the bough.

XXXIV.

SERENADE.

WHO is Silvia? what is she,
　　That all our swains commend her?
Holy, fair and wise is she;
　The heaven such grace did lend her,
That she might admired be.

Is she kind as she is fair?
　For beauty lives with kindness:
Love doth to her eyes repair,
　To help him of his blindness;
And, being helped, inhabits there.

Then to Silvia let us sing,
　That Silvia is excelling;
She excels each mortal thing
　Upon the dull earth dwelling;
To her let us garlands bring.

XXXV.

AMIENS' SONG. I.

U NDER the greenwood tree
    Who loves to lie with me,
And turn his merry note
Unto the sweet bird's throat,
Come hither, come hither, come hither:
    Here shall he see
    No enemy
But winter and rough weather.

Who doth ambition shun,
    And loves to live i' the sun,
    Seeking the food he eats,
    And pleased with what he gets,
Come hither, come hither, come hither:
    Here shall he see
    No enemy
But winter and rough weather.

XXXVI.

AMIENS' SONG. II.

B LOW, blow, thou winter wind,
   Thou art not so unkind
As man's ingratitude ;
Thy tooth is not so keen,
Because thou art not seen,
   Although thy breath be rude.
Heigh ho ! sing, heigh ho ! unto the green holly :
Most friendship is feigning, most loving mere folly.
   Then, heigh ho, the holly !
   This life is most jolly.

Freeze, freeze, thou bitter sky,
That dost not bite so nigh
   As benefits forgot :
Though thou the waters warp,
Thy sting is not so sharp
   As friend remembered not.
Heigh ho ! sing, heigh ho ! unto the green holly :
Most friendship is feigning, most loving mere folly.
   Then, heigh ho, the holly !
   This life is most jolly.

6

XXXVII.

FESTE, THE JESTER'S SONG. I.

O MISTRESS mine ! where are you roaming?
O ! stay and hear ; your true love's coming,
That can sing both high and low.
Trip no further, pretty sweeting ;
Journeys end in lovers meeting,
Every wise man's son doth know.

What is love ? 'tis not hereafter ;
Present mirth hath present laughter ;
What's to come is still unsure :
In delay there lies no plenty ;
Then come kiss me, sweet-and-twenty,
Youth's a stuff will not endure.

XXXVIII.

FESTE, THE JESTER'S SONG. II.

COME away, come away, death,
And in sad cypress let me be laid ;
Fly away, fly away, breath ;
I am slain by a fair cruel maid.

My shroud of white, stuck all with yew,
   O ! prepare it :
My part of death, no one so true
    Did share it.

Not a flower, not a flower sweet,
 On my black coffin let there be strown ;
Not a friend, not a friend greet
 My poor corse, where my bones shall be thrown :
A thousand thousand sighs to save,
    Lay me, O ! where
Sad true lover never find my grave,
    To weep there.

XXXIX.

SONG.

ORPHEUS with his lute made trees,
  And the mountain tops that freeze,
 Bow themselves, when he did sing :
To his music plants and flowers
Ever sprung ; as sun and showers
 There had made a lasting spring.

Every thing that heard him play,
Even the billows of the sea,
 Hung their heads, and then lay by.

In sweet music is such art,
Killing care and grief of heart
Fall asleep, or hearing, die.

XL.

SERENADE.

H ARK, hark ! the lark at heaven's gate sings,
    And Phœbus 'gins arise,
His steeds to water at those springs
    On chaliced flowers that lies ;
And winking Mary-buds begin
    To ope their golden eyes :
With every thing that pretty is,
    My lady sweet, arise :
        Arise, arise.

XLI.

A DIRGE.

F EAR no more the heat o' the sun,
    Nor the furious winter's rages ;
Thou thy worldly task hast done,
    Home art gone, and ta'en thy wages :
Golden lads and girls all must,
As chimney-sweepers, come to dust.

Fear no more the frown o' the great ;
  Thou art past the tyrant's stroke ;
Care no more to clothe and eat ;
  To thee the reed is as the oak :
The sceptre, learning, physic, must
All follow this, and come to dust.

Fear no more the lightning-flash,
  Nor the all-dreaded thunder-stone ;
Fear not slander, censure rash ;
  Thou hast finished joy and moan :
All lovers young, all lovers must
Consign to thee, and come to dust.

  No exorciser harm thee !
  Nor no witchcraft charm thee !
  Ghost unlaid forbear thee !
  Nothing ill come near thee !
  Quiet consummation have ;
  And renowned be thy grave !

XLII.

YOUTH AND AGE.

CRABBED age and youth cannot live together :
    Youth is full of pleasance, age is full of care ;
Youth like summer morn, age like winter weather ;
    Youth like summer brave, age like winter bare.
Youth is full of sport, age's breath is short ;
    Youth is nimble, age is lame ;
Youth is hot and bold, age is weak and cold ;
    Youth is wild, and age is tame.
Age, I do abhor thee ; youth, I do adore thee ;
    O ! my love, my love is young.
Age, I do defy thee : O ! sweet shepherd, hie thee,
    For methinks thou stayest too long.

Sir Henry Wotton,
1568—1639.

XLIII.

THE CHARACTER OF A HAPPY LIFE.

HOW happy is he born and taught,
   That serveth not another's will;
Whose armour is his honest thought,
   And simple truth his utmost skill!

Whose passions not his masters are;
   Whose soul is still prepared for death,
Untied unto the world by care
   Of public fame, or private breath;

Who envies none that chance doth raise,
   Nor vice; who never understood
How deepest wounds are given by praise;
   Nor rules of state, but rules of good;

Who hath his life from rumours freed;
   Whose conscience is his strong retreat;
Whose state can neither flatterers feed,
   Nor ruin make oppressors great:

Who God doth late and early pray
  More of his grace than gifts to lend ;
And entertains the harmless day
  With a religious book or friend.

This man is freed from servile bands
  Of hope to rise, or fear to fall ;
Lord of himself, though not of lands ;
  And having nothing, yet hath all.

THOMAS DEKKER,
1570?—1638?

XLIV.

SONG.

ART thou poor, yet hast thou golden slumbers:
      O sweet content!
Art thou rich, yet is thy mind perplexed?
      O punishment.
Dost thou laugh to see how fools are vexed?
To add to golden numbers, golden numbers.
      O sweet content, O sweet content.
Work apace, apace, apace, apace,
Honest labour bears a lovely face,
Then hey nonny, nonny: hey nonny, nonny.

Canst drink the waters of the crisped spring,
      O sweet content!
Swim'st thou in wealth, yet sink'st in thine own tears,
      O punishment.
Then he that patiently want's burden bears,
No burden bears, but is a king, a king.
      O sweet content, O sweet content.
Work apace, apace, apace, apace,
Honest labour bears a lovely face,
Then hey nonny, nonny: hey nonny, nonny.

XLV.   JOHN WEBSTER.

CORNELIA'S SONG.

CALL for the robin-red-breast and the wren,
  Since o'er shady groves they hover,
And with leaves and flowers do cover
The friendless bodies of unburied men.
Call unto his funeral dole
The ant, the field-mouse, and the mole,
To rear him hillocks that shall keep him warm,
And, when gay tombs are robbed, sustain no harm ;
But keep the wolf far thence, that's foe to men,
For with his nails he'll dig them up again.
Let holy church receive him duly,
Since he paid the church tithes truly.

XLVI.

JOHN DONNE,
1573—1631.

THE MESSAGE.

SEND home my long-strayed eyes to me,
  Which, oh ! too long have dwelt on thee ;
But if there they have learnt such ill,
    Such forced fashions
    And false passions,
      That they be
      Made by thee
Fit for no good sight, keep them still.

Send home my harmless heart again,
Which no unworthy thought could stain ;
But if it be taught by thine
    To make jestings
    Of protestings,
      And break both
      Word and oath,
Keep it, for then 'tis none of mine.

Yet send me back my heart and eyes,
That I may know and see thy lies,

And may laugh and joy when thou
    Art in anguish,
    And dost languish
        For some one
        That will none,
Or prove as false as thou dost now.

XLVII.

VALEDICTION, FORBIDDING MOURNING.

AS virtuous men pass mildly away,
    And whisper to their souls to go ;
Whilst some of their sad friends do say,
    Now his breath goes, and some say, no ;

So let us melt, and make no noise,
    No tear-floods nor sigh-tempests move ;
'Twere profanation of our joys
    To tell the laity our love.

Moving of the earth brings harms and fears,
    Men reckon what it did, and meant ;
But trepidations of the spheres,
    Though greater far, are innocent.

Dull sublunary lovers' love,
  Whose soul is sense, cannot admit
Absence ; for that it doth remove
  Those things which elemented it.

But we, by a love so far refined,
  That ourselves know not what it is,
Inter-assured of the mind,
  Careless, eyes, lips, and hands to miss.

Our two souls therefore, which are one,
  Though I must go, endure not yet
A breach, but an expansion,
  Like gold to airy thinness beat.

If they be two, they are two so
  As stiff twin compasses are two ;
Thy soul, the fixed foot, makes no show
  To move, but doth if the other do.

And though it in the centre sit,
  Yet when the other far doth roam,
It leans and hearkens after it,
  And grows erect as that comes home.

Such wilt thou be to me, who must,
  Like the other foot, obliquely run ;
Thy firmness makes my circles just,
  And makes me end where I begun.

XLVIII.

A HYMN TO GOD THE FATHER.

WILT Thou forgive that sin where I begun,
　　Which was my sin, though it were done before?
Wilt Thou forgive that sin, through which I run
　　And do run still, though still I do deplore?
When Thou hast done, Thou hast not done;
　　　　For I have more.

Wilt Thou forgive that sin which I have won
　　Others to sin, and made my sins their door?
Wilt Thou forgive that sin which I did shun
　　A year or two, but wallowed in, a score?
When Thou hast done, Thou hast not done;
　　　　For I have more.

I have a sin of fear, that when I have spun
　　My last thread, I shall perish on the shore;
But swear by Thyself, that at my death Thy Son
　　Shall shine, as He shines now and heretofore:
And having done that, Thou hast done;
　　　　I fear no more.

XLIX.

THE FUNERAL.

WHOEVER comes to shroud me, do not harm
   Nor question much
That subtle wreath of hair about mine arm ;
The mystery, the sign you must not touch,
  For 'tis my outward soul,
Viceroy to that which, then to heaven being gone,
  Will leave this to control
And keep these limbs, her provinces, from dissolution.

  For if the sinewy thread my brain lets fall
   Through every part
Can tie those parts, and make me one of all,
The hairs, which upward grew, and strength and art
  Have from a better brain,
Can better do't : except she meant that I
  By this should know my pain,
As prisoners then are manacled, when they're condemned
  to die.

  Whate'er she meant by 't, bury it with me !
   For since I am

Love's martyr, it might breed idolatry
If into other hands these relics came.
  As 'twas humility
To afford to it all that a soul can do,
  So 'tis some bravery
That, since you would have none of me, I bury some of you.

L.
BEN JONSON,
1573—1637.

HESPERUS' SONG.

QUEEN and huntress, chaste and fair,
Now the sun is laid to sleep ;
Seated in thy silver chair,
State in wonted manner keep.
  Hesperus entreats thy light,
  Goddess excellently bright.

Earth, let not thy envious shade
Dare itself to interpose ;
Cynthia's shining orb was made
Heaven to clear, when day did close ;
  Bless us then with wished sight,
  Goddess excellently bright.

Lay thy bow of pearl apart,
And thy crystal-shining quiver ;
Give unto the flying hart
Space to breathe, how short soever:
  Thou that makest a day of night, .
  Goddess excellently bright.

7

LI.

CRISPINUS' AND HERMOGENES' SONG

IF I freely can discover
    What would please me in my lover:
I would have her fair and witty,
Savouring more of court than city;
A little proud, but full of pity:
Light and humorous in her toying,
Oft building hopes, and soon destroying;
Long, but sweet in the enjoying;
Neither too easy, nor too hard:
All extremes I would have barred.

She should be allowed her passions,
So they were but used as fashions;
    Sometimes froward, and then frowning,
    Sometimes sickish, and then swooning,
    Every fit with change still crowning.
    Purely jealous I would have her,
    Then only constant when I crave her.
    'Tis a virtue should not save her.
Thus, nor her delicates would cloy me,
Neither her peevishness annoy me.

LII.

CLERIMONT'S SONG.

STILL to be neat, still to be drest,
  As you were going to a feast ;
Still to be powdered, still perfumed :
Lady, it is to be presumed,
Though art's hid causes are not found,
All is not sweet, all is not sound.

Give me a look, give me a face,
That makes simplicity a grace ;
Robes loosely flowing, hair as free ;
Such sweet neglect more taketh me
Than all the adulteries of art :
They strike mine eyes, but not my heart.

LIII.

AN EPITAPH ON SALATHIEL PAVY, A CHILD OF QUEEN ELIZABETH'S CHAPEL.

WEEP with me all you that read
      This little story ;
And know, for whom a tear you shed
      Death's self is sorry.

'Twas a child that so did thrive
    In grace and feature,
As Heaven and Nature seemed to strive
    Which owned the creature.
Years he numbered scarce thirteen
    When Fates turned cruel,
Yet three filled zodiacs had he been
    The stage's jewel ;
And did act, what now we moan,
    Old men so duly,
As, sooth, the Parcæ thought him one,
    He played so truly.
So, by error to his fate
    They all consented ;
But viewing him since, alas ! too late,
    They have repented ;
And have sought, to give new birth,
    In baths to steep him ;
But being so much too good for earth,
    Heaven vows to keep him.

LIV.

VOLPONE'S SONG.

COME my Celia, let us prove,
    While we may, the sports of love;
Time will not be ours for ever:
He at length our good will sever.
Spend not then his gifts in vain.
Suns that set may rise again:
But if once we lose this light,
'Tis with us perpetual night.
Why should we defer our joys?
Fame and rumour are but toys.
Cannot we delude the eyes
Of a few poor household spies?
Or his easier ears beguile,
So removed by our wile?
'Tis no sin love's fruit to steal,
But the sweet theft to reveal:
To be taken, to be seen,
These have crimes accounted been.

LV.

TO CELIA.

DRINK to me only with thine eyes,
  And I will pledge with mine ;
Or leave a kiss but in the cup,
  And I'll not look for wine.
The thirst that from the soul doth rise,
  Doth ask a drink divine ;
But might I of Jove's nectar sup,
  I would not change for thine.

I sent thee late a rosy wreath,
  Not so much honouring thee,
As giving it a hope that there
  It could not withered be.
But thou thereon did'st only breathe,
  And sent'st it back to me ;
Since when it grows, and smells, I swear,
  Not of itself, but thee.

LVI.

A NYMPH'S PASSION.

I LOVE, and he loves me again,
   Yet dare I not tell who;
For if the nymphs should know my swain,
   I fear they'd love him too;
      Yet if it be not known,
   The pleasure is as good as none,
For that's a narrow joy is but our own.

I'll tell, that if they be not glad,
   They yet may envy me:
But then if I grow jealous mad,
   And of·them pitied be,
      It were a plague 'bove scorn,
   And yet it cannot be forborn,
Unless my heart would as my thought be torn.

He is, if they can find him, fair,
   And fresh and fragrant too,
As summer's sky, or purged air,
   And looks as lilies do
      That are this morning blown;
   Yet, yet I doubt he is not known,
And fear much more, that more of him be shown.

But he hath eyes so round and bright,
    As make away my doubt,
Where Love may all his torches light
    Though Hate had put them out:
        But then to increase my fears,
        What nymph soe'er his voice but hears,
    Will be my rival, though she have but ears.

I'll tell no more, and yet I love,
    And he loves me ; yet no
One unbecoming thought doth move
    From either heart I know ;
        But so exempt from blame,
        As it would be to each a fame,
    If love or fear would let me tell his name.

LVII.

IN CELEBRATION OF CHARIS.
HER TRIUMPH.

SEE the chariot at hand here of Love,
        Wherein my lady rideth !
Each that draws is a swan or a dove,
    And well the car Love guideth.
As she goes, all hearts do duty
            Unto her beauty ;

And enamoured, do wish so they might
      But enjoy such a sight ;
That they still were to run by her side,
Through swords, through seas, whither she would ride.

Do but look on her eyes, they do light
    All that Love's world compriseth !
Do but look on her hair, it is bright
    As Love's star when it riseth !
Do but mark her forehead's smoother
       Than words that soothe her !
And from her arched brows, such a grace
       Sheds itself through the face,
As alone there triumphs to the life
All the gain, all the good of the elements' strife.

Have you seen but a bright lily grow
    Before rude hands have touched it ?
Ha' you marked but the fall o' the snow
    Before the soil hath smutched it ?
Ha' you felt the wool of beaver ?
       Or swan's down ever ?
Or have smelt o' the bud o' the brier ?
       Or the nard in the fire ?
Or have tasted the bag of the bee ?
O so white ! O so soft ! O so sweet is she !

LVIII.

THE DEDICATION OF THE KING'S NEW CELLAR TO BACCHUS.

SINCE, Bacchus, thou art father
    Of wines, to thee the rather
We dedicate this cellar,
Where new, thou art made dweller;
And seal thee thy commission:
But 'tis with a condition,
That thou remain here taster
Of all to the great master.
And look unto their faces,
Their qualities and races,
That both their odour take him,
And relish merry make him.
    For, Bacchus, thou art freer
Of cares, and overseer
Of feast and merry meeting,
And still begin'st the greeting:
See then thou dost attend him,
Lyæus, and defend him,
By all the arts of gladness
From any thought like sadness.
    So may'st thou still be younger

Than Phœbus, and much stronger,
To give mankind their eases,
And cure the world's diseases :
  So may the Muses follow
Thee still, and leave Apollo
And think thy stream more quicker
Than Hippocrene's liquor :
And thou make many a poet
Before his brain do know it ;
So may there never quarrel
Have issue from the barrel ;
But Venus and the Graces
Pursue thee in all places,
And not a song be other
Than Cupid and his mother.

  That when King James above here
Shall feast it, thou may'st love there
The causes and the guests too,
And have thy tales and jests too,
Thy circuits and thy rounds free,
As shall the feast's fair grounds be.
  Be it he hold communion
In great Saint George's union ;
Or gratulates the passage
Of some well-wrought embassage :
Whereby he may knit sure up
The wished peace of Europe :

Or else a health advances,
To put his Court in dances,
And set us all on skipping,
When with his royal shipping
The narrow seas are shady,
And Charles brings home the lady.

Accessit fervor capiti, numerusque lucernis.

RICHARD BARNFIELD,
1574—1627.

LIX.

A S it fell upon a day,
   In the merry month of May,
Sitting in a pleasant shade,
Which a grove of myrtles made.
Beasts did leap, and birds did sing,
Trees did grow, and plants did spring :
Every thing did banish moan,
Save the nightingale alone.
She poor bird, as all forlorn,
Leaned her breast against a thorn,
And there sung the dolefull'st ditty,
That to hear it was great pity.
Fie, fie, fie, now would she cry
Teru, teru, by and by.
That to hear her so complain,
Scarce I could from tears refrain.
For her griefs so lively shown,
Made me think upon mine own.
Ah ! thought I, thou mourn'st in vain,
None takes pity on thy pain.
Senseless trees, they cannot hear thee,
  Ruthless beasts, they will not cheer thee.

King Pandion he is dead,
All thy friends are lapped in lead.
All thy fellow birds do sing,
Careless of thy sorrowing.
Even so poor bird like thee,
None alive will pity me.

THOMAS HEYWOOD,
1575?—1650?

LX.

A MESSAGE TO PHILLIS.

YE little birds that sit and sing
   Amidst the shady valleys,
And see how Phillis sweetly walks
   Within her garden alleys;
Go pretty birds about her bower,
Sing pretty birds, she may not lower,
   Ah me ! methinks I see her frown,
     Ye pretty wantons warble.

Go tell her through your chirping bills,
   As you by me are bidden,
To her is only known my love,
   Which from the world is hidden:
Go pretty birds and tell her so,
See that your notes strain not too low,
   For still methinks I see her frown,
     Ye pretty wantons warble.

Go tune your voices harmony,
   And sing I am her lover;

Strain loud and sweet, that every note,
　With sweet content may move her:
And she that hath the sweetest voice,
Tell her I will not change my choice,
　Yet still methinks I see her frown,
　　Ye pretty wantons warble.

O fly, make haste, see, see, she falls
　Into a pretty slumber,
Sing round about her rosy bed,
　That waking she may wonder ;
Say to her, 'tis her lover true,
That sendeth love to you, to you ;
　And when you have heard her kind reply,
　　Return with pleasant warblings.

LXI.

VALERIUS' SONG.

PACK clouds away, and welcome day,
　　With night we banish sorrow ;
Sweet air blow soft, mount lark aloft,
　To give my love good-morrow.
Wings from the wind to please her mind,
　Notes from the lark I'll borrow ;

Bird prune thy wing, nightingale sing ;
  To give my love good-morrow.
  To give my love good-morrow,
  Notes from them all I 'll borrow.

Wake from thy nest, robin-red-breast,
  Sing birds in every furrow ;
And from each bill, let music shrill,
  Give my fair love good-morrow.
Blackbird and thrush, in every bush,
  Stare, linnet, and cock-sparrow ;
You pretty elves, amongst yourselves,
  Sing my fair love good-morrow.
  To give my love good-morrow,
  Sing birds in every furrow.

8

JOHN FLETCHER,
1576—1625.
FRANCIS BEAUMONT,
1586—1615.

LXII.

ORIANA'S SONG.

COME sleep, and with thy sweet deceiving,
   Lock me in delight awhile;
Let some pleasing dreams beguile
All my fancies; that from thence,
I may feel an influence,
All my powers of care bereaving !

Though but a shadow, but a sliding,
   Let me know some little joy !
We that suffer long annoy
Are contented with a thought,
Through an idle fancy wrought :
Oh ! let my joys have some abiding.

LXIII.

SONG OF THE PRIEST OF PAN.

S HEPHERDS all, and maidens fair,
    Fold your flocks up, for the air
'Gins to thicken, and the sun
Already his great course hath run.
See the dew-drops how they kiss
Every little flower that is ;
Hanging on their velvet heads,
Like a rope of crystal beads ;
See the heavy clouds low falling,
And bright Hesperus down calling
The dead night from under ground ;
At whose rising mists unsound,
Damps and vapours fly apace,
Hovering o'er the wanton face
Of these pastures, where they come
Striking dead both bud and bloom :
Therefore from such danger lock
Every one his loved flock ;
And let your dogs lie loose without,
Lest the wolf come as a scout
From the mountain, and, ere day,

Bear a lamb or kid away;
Or the crafty thievish fox
Break upon your simple flocks.
To secure yourselves from these,
Be not too secure in ease;
Let one eye his watches keep
While the other eye doth sleep;
So you shall good shepherds prove,
And for ever hold the love
Of our great god.   Sweetest slumbers,
And soft silence, fall in numbers
On your eye-lids! So, farewell!
Thus I end my evening's knell.

LXIV.

SONG TO PAN.

ALL ye woods, and trees, and bowers,
All ye virtues and ye powers
That inhabit in the lakes,
In the pleasant springs or brakes,
       Move your feet
       To our sound,
       Whilst we greet
       All this ground,

With his honour and his name
That defends our flocks from blame.

He is great and he is just,
He is ever good, and must
Thus be honoured.   Daffodilies,
Roses, pinks, and loved lilies,
                Let us fling,
                Whilst we sing,
                Ever holy,
                Ever holy,
Ever honoured, ever young !
Thus great Pan is ever sung.

LXV.

SONG.

AWAY, delights, go seek some other dwelling,
                For I must die ;
Farewell, false Love ; thy tongue is ever telling
                Lie after lie.
For ever let me rest now from thy smarts ;
                Alas ! for pity go,
                And fire their hearts
That have been hard to thee ; mine was not so.

Never again deluding Love shall know me,
        For I will die;
And all those griefs that think to over-grow me,
        Shall be as I:
For ever will I sleep, while poor maids cry,
        'Alas! for pity stay,
        And let us die
With thee; men cannot mock us in the clay.'

LXVI.

SONG.

GOD Lyæus, ever young,
    Ever honoured, ever sung;
Stained with blood of lusty grapes,
In a thousand lusty shapes,
Dance upon the mazer's brim,
In the crimson liquor swim;
From thy plenteous hand divine,
Let a river run with wine.
    God of youth, let this day here
    Enter neither care nor fear!

LXVII.

THE PASSIONATE LORD'S SONG.

HENCE, all you vain delights,
 As short as are the nights
  Wherein you spend your folly!
There's nought in this life sweet,
If man were wise to see't,
  But only melancholy;
  Oh! sweetest melancholy.

Welcome, folded arms, and fixed eyes,
A sigh that piercing mortifies,
A look that's fastened to the ground,
A tongue chained up, without a sound!

Fountain heads, and pathless groves,
Places which pale passion loves!
Moonlight walks, when all the fowls
Are warmly housed, save bats and owls!
  A midnight bell, a parting groan!
  These are the sounds we feed upon;
Then stretch our bones in a still gloomy valley;
Nothing's so dainty sweet as lovely melancholy.

LXVIII.

ASPATIA'S SONG.

L AY a garland on my hearse,
    Of the dismal yew;
Maidens, willow branches bear;
    Say I died true;
My love was false, but I was firm
    From my hour of birth.
Upon my buried body lie
    Lightly, gentle earth!

THOMAS MIDDLETON,
1580?—1627.

LXIX.

HIPPOLITO'S SONG.

L OVE is like a lamb, and love is like a lion;
Fly from love, he fights; fight, then does he fly on.
Love is all on fire, and yet is ever freezing;
Love is much in winning, yet is more in leesing;
Love is ever sick, and yet is never dying;
Love is ever true, and yet is ever lying;
Love does dote in liking, and is mad in loathing;
Love indeed is anything, yet indeed is nothing.

LXX.   PHINEAS FLETCHER,
1581—1650.

A HYMN.

DROP, drop, slow tears,
   And bathe those beauteous feet,
Which brought from heaven
   The news and Prince of peace :
Cease not, wet eyes,
   His mercies to entreat ;
To cry for vengeance
   Sin doth never cease :
In your deep floods
   Drown all my faults and fears ;
Nor let his eye
   See sin, but through my tears.

THOMAS CAREW,
1589 ?—1639.

LXXI.

SONG.

A SK me no more where Jove bestows,
   When June is past, the fading rose ;
For in your beauty's orient deep
These flowers, as in their causes, sleep.

Ask me no more whither do stray
The golden atoms of the day ;
For, in pure love, heaven did prepare
Those powders to enrich your hair.

Ask me no more whither doth haste
The nightingale when May is past ;
For in your sweet dividing throat
She winters and keeps warm her note.

Ask me no more where those stars light
That downwards fall in dead of night ;
For in your eyes they sit, and there
Fixed become as in their sphere.

Ask me no more if east or west
The phœnix builds her spicy nest ;
For unto you at last she flies,
And in your fragrant bosom dies.

GEORGE WITHER,
1590?—1667.

LXXII.

THE SHEPHERD'S RESOLUTION.

S HALL I, wasting in despair,
   Die because a woman's fair?
Or make pale my cheeks with care,
'Cause another's rosy are?
Be she fairer than the day,
Or the flowery meads in May;
   If she be not so to me
   What care I how fair she be?

Should my heart be grieved or pined,
'Cause I see a woman kind?
Or a well-disposed nature
Joined with a lovely feature?
Be she meeker kinder than
Turtle dove or pelican,
   If she be not so to me,
   What care I how kind she be?

Shall a woman's virtues move
Me to perish for her love?

Or her well-deserving known
Make me quite forget mine own?
Be she with that goodness blest,
Which may gain her name of best,
   If she be not such to me,
   What care I how good she be?

'Cause her fortune seems too high,
Shall I play the fool and die?
Those that bear a noble mind,
Where they want of riches find,
Think what with them they would do,
That without them dare to woo,
   And unless that mind I see,
   What care I, though great she be?

Great or good, or kind, or fair,
I will ne'er the more despair;
If she love me, this believe
I will die ere she shall grieve.
If she slight me when I woo,
I can scorn and let her go,
   For if she be not for me,
   What care I for whom she be?

ROBERT HERRICK,
1591—1674.

LXXIII.

THE CHEAT OF CUPID; OR, THE UNGENTLE GUEST.

ONE silent night of late,
  When every creature rested,
Came one unto my gate,
  And knocking, me molested.

Who's that, said I, beats there,
  And troubles thus the sleepy?
Cast off, said he, all fear;
  And let not locks thus keep ye.

For I a boy am, who
  By moonless nights have swerved;
And all with showers wet through,
  And e'en with cold half starved.

I pitiful arose,
  And soon a taper lighted;
And did myself disclose
  Unto the lad benighted.

I saw he had a bow,
  And wings too, which did shiver;
And looking down below,
  I spied he had a quiver.

I to my chimney's shine
  Brought him, as love professes,
And chafed his hands with mine,
  And dried his dropping tresses:

But when he felt him warmed,
  Let's try this bow of ours,
And string, if they be harmed,
  Said he, with these late showers.

Forthwith his bow he bent,
  And wedded string and arrow,
And struck me, that it went
  Quite through my heart and marrow.

Then laughing loud, he flew
  Away, and thus said flying,
Adieu, mine host, adieu,
  I'll leave thy heart a-dying.

LXXIV.

THE TEAR.

GLIDE, gentle streams, and bear
   Along with you my tear
To that coy girl ;
   Who smiles, yet slays
   Me with delays,
And strings my tears as pearl.

See ! see ! she's yonder set,
Making a carcanet
   Of maiden flowers :
   There, there present
   This orient,
And pendant· pearl of ours.

Then say, I've sent one more
Gem to enrich her store ;
   And that is all
   Which I can send
   Or vainly spend,
For tears no more will fall.

Nor will I seek supply
Of them, the springs once dry ;
9

But I'll devise,
  Among the rest,
  A way that's best
How I may save mine eyes.

Yet say, should she condemn
Me to surrender them ;
  Then say, my part
    Must be to weep
    Out them, to keep
  A poor yet loving heart.

Say too, she would have this :
She shall.   Then my hope is
  That when I'm poor,
    And nothing have
    To send or save,
  I'm sure she'll ask no more.

LXXV.

TO THE VIRGINS, TO MAKE MUCH OF TIME.

GATHER ye rose-buds while ye may,
    Old Time is still a-flying :
And this same flower that smiles to day
To-morrow will be dying.

The glorious lamp of heaven, the sun,
   The higher he's a-getting;
The sooner will his race be run,
   And nearer he's to setting.

That age is best, which is the first,
   When youth and blood are warmer;
But being spent, the worse, and worst
   Times, still succeed the former.

Then be not coy, but use your time;
   And while ye may, go marry:
For having lost but once your prime,
   You may for ever tarry.

LXXVI.

HIS POETRY HIS PILLAR.

O NLY a little more
    I have to write,
Then I'll give o'er,
   And bid the world good-night.

'Tis but a flying minute,
   That I must stay,
Or linger in it;
   And then I must away.

O time that cutt'st down all !
   And scarce leav'st here
Memorial
   Of any men that were.

How many lie forgot
   In vaults beneath ?
And piece-meal rot
   Without a fame in death ?

Behold this living stone,
   I rear for me,
Ne'er to be thrown
   Down, envious Time, by thee.

Pillars let some set up,
   If so they please,
Here is my hope,
   And my *Pyramides.*

LXXVII.

TO MUSIC, TO BECALM HIS FEVER.

CHARM me asleep, and melt me so
   With thy delicious numbers ;
That being ravished, hence I go
   Away in easy slumbers.

Ease my sick head,
And make my bed,
Thou Power that canst sever
From me this ill:
And quickly still:
Though thou not kill
My fever.

Thou sweetly canst convert the same
From a consuming fire,
Into a gentle-licking flame,
And make it thus expire.
Then make me weep
My pains asleep;
And give me such reposes,
That I, poor I,
May think, thereby,
I live and die
'Mongst roses.

Fall on me like a silent dew,
Or like those maiden showers,
Which, by the peep of day, do strew
A baptism o'er the flowers.
Melt, melt my pains,
With thy soft strains;

That having ease me given,
    With full delight,
    I leave this light ;
    And take my flight
    For heaven.

LXXVIII.

TO ANTHEA, WHO MAY COMMAND HIM ANY THING.

B ID me to live, and I will live
        Thy Protestant to be :
Or bid me love, and I will give
    A loving heart to thee.

A heart as soft, a heart as kind,
    A heart as sound and free,
As in the whole world thou canst find,
    That heart I'll give to thee.

Bid that heart stay, and it will stay,
    To honour thy decree :
Or bid it languish quite away,
    And 't shall do so for thee.

Bid me to weep, and I will weep,
　While I have eyes to see :
And having none, yet I will keep
　A heart to weep for thee.

Bid me despair, and I'll despair,
　Under that cypress tree :
Or bid me die, and I will dare
　E'en death, to die for thee.

Thou art my life, my love, my heart,
　The very eyes of me ;
And hast command of every part,
　To live and die for thee.

LXXIX.

TO DAFFODILS.

FAIR daffodils, we weep to see
　　You haste away so soon :
As yet the early-rising sun
　Has not attained his noon.
　　Stay, stay,
　Until the hasting day
　　　Has run

But to the even-song ;
And, having prayed together, we
   Will go with you along.

We have short time to stay, as you,
   We have as short a spring ;
As quick a growth to meet decay,
   As you or any thing.
      We die,
   As your hours do, and dry
         Away,
   Like to the summer's rain ;
Or as the pearls of morning's dew,
   Ne'er to be found again.

LXXX.

THE MAD MAID'S SONG.

GOOD morrow to the day so fair ;
   Good morning, sir, to you :
Good morrow to mine own torn hair
   Bedabbled with the dew.

Good morning to this primrose too ;
   Good morrow to each maid ;
That will with flowers the tomb bestrew,
   Wherein my love is laid.

Ah ! woe is me, woe, woe is me ;
   Alack and well-a-day !
For pity, sir, find out that bee,
   Which bore my love away.

I'll seek him in your bonnet brave ;
   I'll seek him in your eyes ;
Nay, now I think they have made his grave
   I' the bed of strawberries.

I'll seek him there ; I know, ere this,
   The cold, cold earth doth shake him ;
But I will go, or send a kiss
   By you, sir, to awake him.

Pray hurt him not ; though he be dead,
   He knows well who do love him,
And who with green-turfs rear his head,
   And who do rudely move him.

He's soft and tender, pray take heed,
   With bands of cowslips bind him ;
And bring him home ; but 'tis decreed,
   That I shall never find him.

LXXXI.

TO BLOSSOMS.

FAIR pledges of a fruitful tree,
      Why do ye fall so fast ?
      Your date is not so past
But you may stay yet here awhile,
      To blush and gently smile ;
      And go at last.

What, were ye born to be
      An hour or half's delight ;
      And so to bid good-night ?
'Twas pity Nature brought ye forth
      Merely to show your worth
      And lose you quite.

But you are lovely leaves, where we
      May read how soon things have
      Their end, though ne'er so brave :
And after they have shown their pride,
      Like you awhile : They glide
      Into the grave.

LXXXII.

HIS PRAYER TO BEN JONSON.

WHEN I a verse shall make,
　　Know I have prayed thee,
For old religion's sake,
　　Saint Ben to aid me.

Make the way smooth for me,
　　When I, thy Herrick,
Honouring thee, on my knee,
　　Offer my lyric.

Candles I'll give to thee,
　　And a new altar ;
And thou Saint Ben, shalt be
　　Writ in my psalter.

LXXXIII.

THE NIGHT-PIECE, TO JULIA.

HER eyes the glow-worm lend thee,
　　The shooting stars attend thee ;
And the elves also,
Whose little eyes glow,
Like the sparks of fire, befriend thee.

No will-o'-the-wisp mislight thee ;
Nor snake or slow-worm bite thee :
    But on, on thy way
    Not making a stay,
Since ghost there's none to affright thee.

Let not the dark thee cumber ;
What though the moon does slumber?
    The stars of the night
    Will lend thee their light,
Like tapers clear without number.

Then Julia let me woo thee,
Thus, thus to come unto me :
    And when I shall meet
    Thy silvery feet
My soul I'll pour into thee.

LXXXIV.

A TERNARY OF LITTLES, UPON A PIPKIN OF JELLY SENT TO A LADY.

A LITTLE saint best fits a little shrine,
  A little prop best fits a little vine,
As my small cruse best fits my little wine.

A little seed best fits a little soil,
A little trade best fits a little toil :
As my small jar best fits my little oil.

A little bin best fits a little bread,
A little garland fits a little head :
As my small stuft best fits my little shed.

A little hearth best fits a little fire,
A little chapel fits a little choir,
As my small bell best fits my little spire.

A little stream best fits a little boat ;
A little lead best fits a little float ;
As my small pipe best fits my little note.

A little meat best fits a little belly,
As sweetly, lady, give me leave to tell ye,
This little pipkin fits this little jelly.

LXXXV.

AN ODE FOR BEN JONSON.

AH Ben !
      Say how or when
Shall we thy guests
Meet at those lyric feasts
Made at the Sun,

The Dog, the Triple Tun,
Where we such clusters had
As made us nobly wild, not mad?
And yet each verse of thine
Outdid the meat, outdid the frolic wine.

My Ben!
Or come agen,
Or send to us
Thy wit's great overplus.
But teach us yet
Wisely to husband it;
Lest we that talent spend;
And having once brought to an end
That precious stock, the store
Of such a wit the world should have no more.

LXXXVI.

A THANKSGIVING TO GOD FOR HIS HOUSE.

L ORD, thou hast given me a cell
       Wherein to dwell;
And little house, whose humble roof
    Is weather proof;

Under the spars of which I lie
    Both soft and dry.
Where thou, my chamber for to ward,
    Hast set a guard
Of harmless thoughts, to watch and keep
    Me while I sleep.
Low is my porch, as is my fate,
    Both void of state ;
And yet the threshold of my door
    Is worn by the poor,
Who thither come, and freely get
    Good words or meat.
Like as my parlour, so my hall,
    And kitchen small ;
A little buttery, and therein
    A little bin,
Which keeps my little loaf of bread
    Unchipped, unflead.
Some brittle sticks of thorn or brier
    Make me a fire,
Close by whose living coal I sit,
    And glow like it.
Lord, I confess too, when I dine,
    The pulse is thine,
And all those other bits that be
    There placed by thee.
The worts, the purslain, and the mess

Of water-cress,
Which of thy kindness thou hast sent :
    And my content
Makes those, and my beloved beet,
    To be more sweet.
'Tis thou that crown'st my glittering hearth
    With guiltless mirth ;
And giv'st me wassail bowls to drink,
    Spiced to the brink.
Lord, 'tis thy plenty-dropping hand
    That soils my land :
And giv'st me, for my bushel sown,
    Twice ten for one :
Thou mak'st my teeming hen to lay
    Her egg each day :
Besides my healthful ewes to bear
    Me twins each year :
The while the conduits of my kine
    Run cream, for wine.
All these, and better, thou dost send
    Me to this end :
That I should render, for my part
    A thankful heart,
Which, fired with incense, I resign
    As wholly thine :
But the acceptance that must be,
    My Christ, by thee.

HENRY KING.
1592—1669.

LXXXVII.

ON THE LIFE OF MAN.

LIKE to the falling of a star,
　Or as the flights of eagles are,
Or like the fresh spring's gaudy hue,
Or silver drops of morning dew,
Or like a wind that chafes the flood,
Or bubbles which on water stood :
Even such is man, whose borrowed light
Is straight called in and paid to night.

The wind blows out, the bubble dies,
The spring entombed in autumn lies ;
The dew dries up, the star is shot,
The flight is past, and man forgot.

10

GEORGE HERBERT,
1593—1633.

LXXXVIII.

VIRTUE.

S WEET day, so cool, so calm, so bright,   .
   The bridal of the earth and sky,
The dew shall weep thy fall to-night;
      For thou must die.

Sweet rose, whose hue angry and brave
   Bids the rash gazer wipe his eye,
Thy root is ever in its grave,
      And thou must die.

Sweet spring, full of sweet days and roses,
   A box where sweets compacted lie,
My music shows ye have your closes,
      And all must die.

Only a sweet and virtuous soul,
   Like seasoned timber, never gives;
But though the whole world turn to coal,
      Then chiefly lives.

LXXXIX.

MAN'S MEDLEY.

H ARK how the birds do sing,
        And woods do ring :
All creatures have their joy, and man hath his.
    Yet if we rightly measure,
        Man's joy and pleasure
Rather hereafter than in present is.

    To this life things of sense
        Make their pretence ;
In the other angels have a right by birth :   ⟍
    Man ties them both alone,
        And makes them one,
With the one hand touching heaven, with the other earth.

    In soul he mounts and flies,
        In flesh he dies ;
He wears a stuff whose thread is coarse and round,
    But trimmed with curious lace,
        And should take place
After the trimming, not the stuff and ground.

    Not that he may not here
        Taste of the cheer :

But as birds drink, and straight lift up their head,
    So must he sip and think
        Of better drink
He may attain to after he is dead.

    But as his joys are double,
        So is his trouble ;
He hath two winters, other things but one :
    Both frosts and thoughts do nip
        And bite his lip ;
And he of all things fears two deaths alone.

    Yet even the greatest griefs
        May be reliefs,
Could he but take them right and in their ways.
    Happy is he whose heart
        Hath found the art
To turn his double pains to double praise.

XC.

BITTER-SWEET.

AH ! my dear angry Lord,
    Since thou dost love, yet strike,
Cast down, yet help afford ;
    Sure I will do the like.

I will complain, yet praise,
I will bewail, approve ;
And all my sour-sweet days
I will lament, and love.

XCI.

EASTER.

I GOT me flowers to strew thy way,
I got me boughs off many a tree;
But thou wast up by break of day,
And brought'st thy sweets along with thee.

The sun arising in the east,
Though he give light, and the east perfume,
If they should offer to contest
With thy arising, they presume.

Can there be any day but this,
Though many suns to shine endeavour?
We count three hundred, but we miss:
There is but one, and that one ever.

JAMES SHIRLEY,
1594—1666.

XCII.

SERVANT'S SONG.

IF Love his arrows shoot so fast,
  Soon his feathered stock will waste;
But I mistake in thinking so,
Love's arrows in his quiver grow;
How can he want artillery?
That appears too true in me :
Two shafts feed upon my breast,
Oh ! make it quiver for the rest,
Kill me with love, thou angry son
Of Cytherea, or let one,
One sharp golden arrow fly,
To wound her heart for whom I die.
Cupid, if thou be'st a child,
Be no god, or be more mild.

XCIII.

SONG OF THE NUNS.

O, FLY my soul ! What hangs upon
        Thy drooping wings,
        And weighs them down
With love of gaudy mortal things?
The sun is now i' the east ; each shade
        As he doth rise
        Is shorter made,
That earth may lessen to our eyes :
Oh ! be not careless then, and play
        Until the star of peace
Hide all his beams in dark recess.
Poor pilgrims needs must lose their way,
When all the shadows do increase.

XCIV.

SONG OF CALCHAS.

THE glories of our blood and state
        Are shadows, not substantial things ;
There is no armour against fate ;
        Death lays his icy hand on kings :

Sceptre and crown
Must tumble down,
And in the dust be equal made
With the poor crooked scythe and spade.

Some men with swords may reap the field,
  And plant fresh laurels where they kill ;
But their strong nerves at last must yield ;
  They tame but one another still:
      Early or late,
      They stoop to fate,
And must give up their murmuring breath,
When they, pale captives, creep to death.

The garlands wither on your brow,
  Then boast no more your mighty deeds ;
Upon Death's purple altar now,
  See, where the victor-victim bleeds:
      Your heads must come
      To the cold tomb,
Only the actions of the just
Smell sweet, and blossom in their dust.

XCV.   SIMON WASTELL,
                                  circa 1600.

UPON THE IMAGE OF DEATH.

BEFORE my face the picture hangs
   That daily should put me in mind
Of those cold qualms and bitter pangs,
  That shortly I am like to find :
But yet, alas ! full little I
Do think hereon that I must die.

I often look upon the face
  Most ugly, grisly, bare, and thin ;
I often view the hollow place
  Where eyes and nose had sometime been ;
I see the bones, across that lie,
Yet little think that I must die.

I read the label underneath,
  That telleth me whereto I must :
I see the sentence eke that saith
  ' Remember, man, that thou art dust.'
But yet, alas ! but seldom I
Do think indeed that I must die.

Continually at my bed's head
  An hearse doth hang, which doth me tell
That I ere morning may be dead,
  Though now I feel myself full well :
But yet, alas ! for all this I
Have little mind that I must die.

The gown which I do use to wear,
  The knife wherewith I cut my meat,
And eke that old and ancient chair
  Which is my only usual seat,
All these do tell me I must die,
And yet my life amend not I.

My ancestors are turned to clay,
  And many of my mates are gone,
My youngers daily drop away,
  And can I think to 'scape alone ?
No, no, I know that I must die,
And yet my life amend not I.

  If none can 'scape death's dreadful dart,
  If rich and poor his beck obey,
If strong, if wise, if all do smart,
  Then I to 'scape shall have no way.
O grant me grace, O God, that I
My life may mend, sith I must die.

XCVI.

Sir William Davenant,
1605—1668.

SONG.

THE lark now leaves his watery nest,
    And climbing, shakes his dewy wings ;
He takes this window for the east ;
    And to implore your light, he sings,
Awake, awake, the morn will never rise,
Till she can dress her beauty at your eyes.

The merchant bows unto the seaman's star,
    The ploughman from the sun his season takes ;
But still the lover wonders what they are,
    Who look for day before his mistress wakes.
Awake, awake, break through your veils of lawn,
Then draw your curtains, and begin the dawn.

EDMUND WALLER,
1605—1687.

XCVII.

SONG.

G O, lovely rose !
  Tell her that wastes her time, and me,
    That now she knows,
When I resemble her to thee,
How sweet and fair she seems to be.

Tell her that's young,
And shuns to have her graces spied,
    That hadst thou sprung
In deserts, where no men abide,
Thou must have uncommended died.

Small is the worth
Of beauty from the light retired ;
    Bid her come forth,
Suffer herself to be desired,
And not blush so to be admired.

Then die ! that she
The common fate of all things rare
    May read in thee ;
How small a part of time they share
That are so wond'rous sweet and fair.

XCVIII.

JOHN MILTON,
1608—1674.

SONG ON MAY MORNING.

NOW the bright morning star, day's harbinger,
  Comes dancing from the east, and leads with her
The flowery May, who from her green lap throws
The yellow cowslip and the pale primrose.
    Hail bounteous May, that dost inspire
    Mirth and youth and warm desire ;
    Woods and groves are of thy dressing,
    Hill and dale doth boast thy blessing.
Thus we salute thee with our early song,
And welcome thee and wish thee long.

XCIX.

THE LADY'S SONG.

SWEET Echo, sweetest nymph, that liv'st unseen
        Within thy airy shell
    By slow Meander's margent green,
And in the violet-embroidered vale,
        Where the love-lorn nightingale

Nightly to thee her sad song mourneth well :
Can'st thou not tell me of a gentle pair
          That likest thy Narcissus are ?
          O ! if thou have
    Hid them in some flowery cave,
          Tell me but where,
    Sweet queen of parley, daughter of the sphere,
    So may'st thou be translated to the skies,
And give resounding grace to all heaven's harmonies.

SIR JOHN SUCKLING,
1609—1641.

C.

ORSAMES' SONG.

WHY so pale and wan, fond lover?
    Prithee, why so pale?
Will, when looking well can't move her,
    Looking ill prevail?
    Prithee, why so pale?

Why so dull and mute, young sinner?
    Prithee, why so mute?
Will, when speaking well can't win her,
    Saying nothing do 't?
    Prithee, why so mute?

Quit, quit, for shame! this will not move,
    This cannot take her;
If of herself she will not love,
    Nothing can make her:
    The devil take her!

CI.

SONG.

HONEST lover whosoever,
    If in all thy love there ever
Was one wavering thought, if thy flame
Were not still even, still the same :
        Know this,
        Thou lovest amiss,
And to love true,
Thou must begin again, and love anew.

If when she appears i' the room
Thou dost not quake, and art struck dumb,
And in striving this to cover
Dost not speak thy words twice over,
        Know this,
        Thou lovest amiss,
And to love true,
Thou must begin again, and love anew.

If fondly thou dost not mistake,
And all defects for graces take,

Persuad'st thyself that jests are broken
When she hath little or nothing spoken,
    Know this,   *
    Thou lovest amiss,
And to love true,
Thou must begin again, and love anew.

If when thou appear'st to be within
Thou lett'st not men ask and ask again ;
And when thou answerest, if it be
To what was asked thee, properly,
    Know this,
    Thou lovest amiss,
And to love true,
Thou must begin again, and love anew.

If when thy stomach calls to eat
Thou cutt'st not fingers 'stead of meat,
And with much gazing on her face
Dost not rise hungry from the place,
    Know this,
    Thou lovest amiss,
And to love true,
Thou must begin again, and love anew.

If by this thou dost discover
That thou art no perfect lover,
  II

And desiring to love true,
Thou dost begin to love anew,
        Know this,
        Thou lovest amiss,
And to love true,
Thou must begin again, and love anew.

RICHARD CRASHAW,
1612—1649.

CII.

ON THE ASSUMPTION.

HARK ! she is called, the parting hour is come ;
  Take thy farewell, poor world ! Heaven must go
  home. .
A piece of heavenly earth ; purer and brighter
Than the chaste stars, whose choice lamps come to light
    her,
Whil'st through the crystal orbs, clearer than they,
She climbs ; and makes a far more milky way.
She's called. Hark how the dear immortal dove
Sighs to his silver mate, ' Rise up,' my love,

        Rise up, my fair, my spotless one,
        The winter's past, the rain is gone ;
        The spring is come, the flowers appear,
        No sweets, save thou, are wanting here.

            Come away, my love,
            Come away, my dove,
              Cast off delay ;
            The court of heaven is come
            To wait upon thee home ;
              Come, come away !

The flowers appear,
Or quickly would, wert thou once here.
The spring is come, or if it stay
'Tis to keep time with thy delay.
The rain is gone, except so much as we
Detain in needful tears to weep the want of thee.
. The winter's past,
Or if he make less haste,
His answer is, Why, she does so ;
If summer come not, how can winter go ?
Come away, come away !
The shrill winds chide, the waters weep thy stay,
The fountains murmur, and each loftiest tree
Bows lowest his leafy top to look for thee.
Come away, my love,
Come away, my dove,
Cast off delay ;
The court of heaven is come
To wait upon thee home ;
Come, come away.

She's called again.   And will she go ?
When heaven bids come, who can say no ?
Heaven calls her, and she must away,
Heaven will not, and she cannot stay.
Go then ; go, glorious on the golden wings
Of the bright youth of heaven, that sings

Under so sweet a burden.   Go,
Since thy dread son will have it so.
And while thou goest, our song and we
Will, as we may, reach after thee.

  Hail, holy queen of humble hearts !
  We in thy praise will have our parts.
And though thy dearest looks must now give light
To none but the blest heavens, whose bright
Beholders, lost in sweet delight,
Feed for ever their fair sight
With those divinest eyes, which we
And our dark world no more shall see ;
Though our poor eyes are parted so,
Yet shall our lips never let go
Thy gracious name, but to the last
Our loving song shall hold it fast.

  Thy precious name shall be
  Thyself to us, and we
  With holy care will keep it by us.
   We to the last
   Will hold it fast,
  And no Assumption shall deny us.
   All the sweetest showers
   Of our fairest flowers
Will we strow upon it.
   Though our sweets cannot make
   It sweeter, they can take

Themselves new sweetness from it.
Maria, men and angels sing,
Maria, mother of our King.
Live, rosy princess, live, and may the bright
Crown of a most incomparable light
Embrace thy radiant brows.   O may the best
Of everlasting joys bathe thy white breast.

Live, our chaste love, the holy mirth
Of heaven; the humble pride of earth.
Live, crown of women; queen of men;
Live, mistress of our song.   And when
Our weak desires have done their best,
Sweet angels come, and sing the rest.

CIII.

SIR RICHARD LOVELACE,
1618—1658.

TO LUCASTA. GOING BEYOND THE SEAS.

IF to be absent were to be
    Away from thee;
Or that when I am gone,
You or I were alone;
Then my Lucasta might I crave
Pity from blustering wind or swallowing wave.

But I'll not sigh one blast or gale
    To swell my sail,
Or pay a tear to 'suage
The foaming blew-god's rage;
For whether he will let me pass
Or no, I'm still as happy as I was.

Though seas and land betwixt us both,
    Our faith and troth,
Like separated souls,
All time and space controls:
Above the highest sphere we meet,
Unseen, unknown, and greet as angels greet.

So then we do anticipate
    Our after-tate,
And are alive i' the skies,
    If thus our lips and eyes
Can speak like spirits unconfined
In heaven, their earthy bodies left behind.

CIV.

TO LUCASTA. GOING TO THE WARS.

TELL me not, sweet, I am unkind,
        That from the nunnery
Of thy chaste breast and quiet mind
        To war and arms I fly.

True ; a new mistress now I chase,
    The first foe in the field ;
And with a stronger faith embrace
    A sword, a horse, a shield.

Yet this inconstancy is such
    As you too shall adore ;
I could not love thee, dear, so much,
    Loved I not honour more.

CV.

TO ALTHEA; FROM PRISON.

WHEN Love with unconfined wings
   Hovers within my gates,
And my divine Althea brings
   To whisper at the grates ;
When I lie tangled in her hair,
   And fettered to her eye ;
The gods that wanton in the air,
   Know no such liberty.

When flowing cups run swiftly round
   With no allaying Thames,
Our careless heads with roses bound,
   Our hearts with loyal flames ;
When thirsty grief in wine we steep,
   When healths and draughts go free,
Fishes that tipple in the deep,
   Know no such liberty.

When, like committed linnets, I
   With shriller throat shall sing
The sweetness, mercy, majesty,
   And glories of my king ;

When I shall voice aloud, how good
  He is, how great should be ;
Enlarged winds that curl the flood,
  Know no such liberty.

Stone walls do not a prison make,
  Nor iron bars a cage ;
Minds innocent and quiet take
  That for an hermitage ;
If I have freedom in my love,
  And in my soul am free ;
Angels alone that soar above,
  Enjoy such liberty.

CVI.

ANDREW MARVELL,
1620—1678.

BERMUDAS.

WHERE the remote Bermudas ride,
In the ocean's bosom unespyed ;
From a small boat, that rowed along,
The listening winds received this song.

What should we do but sing his praise,
That led us through the watery maze,
Unto an isle so long unknown,
And yet far kinder than our own ?
Where he the huge sea-monsters wracks
That lift the deep upon their backs.
He lands us on a grassy stage,
Safe from the storms, and prelate's rage.
He gave us this eternal spring,
Which here enamels everything ;
And sends the fowls to us in care,
On daily visits through the air.
He hangs in shades the orange bright,
Like golden lamps in a green night.
And does in the pomegranates close,

Jewels more rich than Ormus shows.
He makes the figs our mouths to meet ;
And throws the melons at our feet.
But apples plants of such a price,
No tree could ever bear them twice.
With cedars chosen by his hand,
From Lebanon, he stores the land.
And makes the hollow seas, that roar,
Proclaim the ambergris on shore.
He cast, of which we rather boast,
The Gospel's pearl upon our coast.
And in these rocks for us did frame
A temple, where to sound his name.
Oh ! let our voice his praise exalt,
'Til it arrive at heaven's vault ;
Which, then, perhaps, rebounding, may
Echo beyond the Mexique Bay.

Thus sung they, in the English boat,
An holy and a cheerful note ;
And all the way, to guide their chime,
With falling oars they kept the time.

CVII.

HENRY VAUGHAN,
1621—1695.

THE RETREAT.

HAPPY those early days, when I
 Shined in my angel infancy !
Before I understood this place
Appointed for my second race,
Or taught my soul to fancy ought
But a white, celestial thought ;
When yet I had not walked above
A mile or two, from my first love,
And looking back, at that short space,
Could see a glimpse of his bright face ;
When on some gilded cloud or flower
My gazing soul would dwell an hour,
And in those weaker glories spy
Some shadows of eternity;
Before I taught my tongue to wound
My conscience with a sinful sound,
Or had the black art to dispense
A several sin to every sense,
But felt through all this fleshly dress
Bright shoots of everlastingness.

O how I long to travel back,
And tread again that ancient track!
That I might once more reach that plain,
Where first I left my glorious train;
From whence the enlightened spirit sees
That shady city of palm trees.
But ah! my soul with too much stay
Is drunk, and staggers in the way.
Some men a forward motion love,
But I by backward steps would move;
And when this dust falls to the urn,
In that state I came, return.

CVIII.

PEACE.

M Y soul, there is a country
        Far beyond the stars,
Where stands a winged sentry
    All skilful in the wars;
There, above noise and danger,
    Sweet Peace sits crowned with smiles,
And One born in a manger
    Commands the beauteous files.
He is thy gracious friend
    And, O my soul awake!

Did in pure love descend
   To die here for thy sake;
If thou can'st get but thither,
   There grows the flower of peace,
The rose that cannot wither,
   Thy fortress and thy ease.
Leave then thy foolish ranges,
   For none can thee secure,
But One, who never changes,
   Thy God, thy life, thy cure.

CIX.

THEY are all gone into the world of light !
   And I alone sit lingering here;
Their very memory is fair and bright,
   And my sad thoughts doth clear.

It glows and glitters in my cloudy breast,
   Like stars upon some gloomy grove,
Or those faint beams in which this hill is dressed,
   After the sun's remove.

I see them walking in an air of glory,
   Whose light doth trample on my days ;

My days, which are at best but dull and hoary,
    Mere glimmering and decays.

O holy hope ! and high humility,
    High as the heavens above !
These are your walks, and you have shewed them me
    To kindle my cold love.

Dear, beauteous death ! the jewel of the just,
    Shining no where, but in the dark ;
What mysteries do lie beyond thy dust ;
    Could man outlook that mark !

He that hath found some fledged bird's nest, may know
    At first sight, if the bird be flown ;
But what fair well or grove he sings in now,
    That is to him unknown.

And yet, as angels in some brighter dreams
    Call to the soul, when man doth sleep ;
So some strange thoughts transcend our wonted themes,
    And into glory peep.

If a star were confined into a tomb
    Her captive flames must needs burn there;
But when the hand that locked her up, gives room,
    She'll shine through all the sphere.

O father of eternal life, and all
   Created glories under thee !
Resume thy spirit from this world of thrall
    Into true liberty.

Either disperse these mists, which blot and fill
   My perspective, still, as they pass ;
Or else remove me hence unto that hill,
    Where I shall need no glass.

12

THOMAS STANLEY,
1625?—1678.
CX.

THE RELAPSE.

O H turn away those cruel eyes,
   The stars of my undoing;
Or death in such a bright disguise
   May tempt a second wooing.

Punish their blind and impious pride,
   Who dare contemn thy glory;
It was my fall that deified
   Thy name, and sealed thy story.

Yet no new sufferings can prepare
   A higher praise to crown thee;
Though my first death proclaim thee fair,
   My second will unthrone thee.

Lovers will doubt thou canst entice
   No other for thy fuel,
And if thou burn one victim twice,
   Both think thee poor and cruel.

CXI.

JOHN DRYDEN,
1631—1700.

SONG TO A FAIR YOUNG LADY, GOING OUT OF TOWN IN THE SPRING.

ASK not the cause why sullen spring
    So long delays her flowers to bear;
Why warbling birds forget to sing,
    And winter storms invert the year:
Chloris is gone; and fate provides
To make it spring, where she resides.

Chloris is gone, the cruel fair;
    She cast not back a pitying eye:
But left her lover in despair,
    To sigh, to languish, and to die:
Ah! how can those fair eyes endure
To give the wounds they will not cure.

Great god of love, why hast thou made
    A face that can all hearts command,
That all religions can invade,
    And change the laws of every land?
Where thou hadst placed such power before,
Thou should'st have made her mercy more.

When Chloris to the temple comes,
   Adoring crowds before her fall ;
She can restore the dead from tombs,
   And every life but mine recall.
I only am by Love designed
To be the victim for mankind.

SIR CHARLES SEDLEY,
1639—1701.

CXII.

SONG.

PHILLIS is my only joy,
    Faithless as the winds or seas ;
Sometimes coming, sometimes coy,
    Yet she never fails to please ;
        If with a frown
        I am cast down,
        Phillis smiling,
        And beguiling,
Makes me happier than before.

Though, alas ! too late I find,
    Nothing can her fancy fix ;
Yet the moment she is kind,
    I forgive her all her tricks ;
        Which, though I see,
        I can't get free ;
        She deceiving,
        I believing ;
What need lovers wish for more ?

CXIII.

VICTORIA'S SONG.

AH Chloris ! that I now could sit
      As unconcerned, as when
Your infant beauty could beget
      No pleasure nor no pain.

When I the dawn used to admire,
      And praised the coming day,
I little thought the growing fire
      Must take my rest away.

Your charms in harmless childhood lay,
      Like metals in the mine :
Age from no face took more away,
      Than youth concealed in thine.

But as your charms insensibly
      To their perfection prest,
Fond love as unperceived did fly,
      And in my bosom rest.

My passion with your beauty grew,
      And Cupid at my heart,
Still as his mother favoured you,
      Threw a new flaming dart.

Each gloried in their wanton part :
  To make a lover he
Employed the utmost of his art,
  To make a beauty she.

Though now I slowly bend to love,
  Uncertain of my fate,
If your fair self my chains approve,
  I shall my freedom hate.

Lovers, like dying men, may well
  At first disordered be ;
Since none alive can truly tell
  What fortune they must see.

APHRA BEHN,
1642—1689.

CXIV.

LOVE ARMED.

SONG.

L OVE in fantastic triumph sat,
   Whilst bleeding hearts around him flowed,
For whom fresh pains he did create,
   And strange tyrannic power he showed.
From thy bright eyes he took his fire,
   Which round about in sport he hurled;
But 'twas from mine he took desire
   Enough to undo the amorous world.

From me he took his sighs and tears,
   From thee his pride and cruelty;
From me his languishments and fears,
   And every killing dart from thee;
Thus thou and I the god have armed,
   And set him up a deity;
But my poor heart alone is harmed,
   Whilst thine the victor is, and free.

ANON.
1658.

CXV.

PHILLADA.

O H ! what a pain is love :
    How shall I bear it ?
She will unconstant prove,
    I greatly fear it.
She so torments my mind,
    That my strength faileth,
And wavers with the wind
    As a ship saileth :
Please her the best I may,
She loves still to gainsay :
Alack and well-a-day !
    Phillada flouts me.

All the fair yesterday
    She did pass by me,
She looked another way
    And would not spy me :
I woo'd her for to dine,
    But could not get her ;
Will had her to the wine—
    He might intreat her.

With Daniel she did dance,
On me she looked askance :
Oh ! thrice unhappy chance ;
    Phillada flouts me.

Fair maid ! be not so coy,
    Do not disdain me !
I am my mother's joy :
    Sweet ! entertain me !
She'll give me when she dies
    All that is fitting :
Her poultry and her bees,
    And her goose sitting,
A pair of mattrass beds,
And a bag full of shreds ;
And yet, for all this guedes,
    Phillada flouts me.

She hath a clout of mine,
    Wrought with blue coventry,
Which she keeps for a sign
    Of my fidelity :
But, 'faith, if she flinch,
    She shall not wear it ;
To Tib, my t' other wench,
    I mean to bear it.

And yet it grieves my heart
So soon from her to part:
Death strike me with his dart!
   Phillada flouts me.

Thou shalt eat crudded cream
   All the year lasting,
And drink the crystal stream
   Pleasant in tasting,
Whig and whey whilst thou lust,
   And ramble-berries,
Pie-lid and pastry crust,
   Pears, plums, and cherries;
Thy raiment shall be thin,
Made of a weevil's skin—
Yet all's not worth a pin:
   Phillada flouts me.

Fair maiden! have a care,
   And in time take me;
I can have those as fair,
   If you forsake me:
For Doll the dairy maid
   Laughed at me lately,
And wanton Winifred
   Favours me greatly.

One throws milk on my clothes,
T' other plays with my nose :
What wanting signs are those !
    Phillada flouts me.

I cannot work nor sleep
    At all in season:
Love wounds my heart so deep,
    Without all reason.
I 'gin to pine away
    In my love's shadow,
Like as a fat beast may
    Penned in a meadow.
I shall be dead, I fear,
Within this thousand year:
And all for that my dear
    Phillada flouts me.

MATTHEW PRIOR,
1664—1721.

CXVI.

TO A CHILD OF QUALITY, FIVE YEARS OLD. MDCCIV. THE AUTHOR THEN FORTY.

LORDS, knights, and squires, the numerous band,
 That wear the fair Miss Mary's fetters,
Were summoned by her high command,
 To shew their passions by their letters.

My pen amongst the rest I took,
 Lest those bright eyes that cannot read
Should dart their kindling fires, and look,
 The power they have to be obeyed.

Nor quality, nor reputation,
 Forbid me yet my flame to tell,
Dear five years old befriends my passion,
 And I may write till she can spell.

For while she makes her silk-worms beds,
 With all the tender things, I swear,
Whilst all the house my passion reads,
 In papers round her baby's hair.

She may receive and own my flame,
   For though the strictest prudes should know it,
She'll pass for a most virtuous dame,
   And I for an unhappy poet.

Then too, alas ! when she shall tear
   The lines some younger rival sends,
She'll give me leave to write I fear,
   And we shall still continue friends.

For as our different ages move,
   'Tis so ordained, would fate but mend it !
That I shall be past making love
   When she begins to comprehend it.

CXVII.

AN ODE.

THE merchant, to secure his treasure,
   Conveys it in a borrowed name :
Euphelia serves to grace my measure,
   But Cloe is my real flame.

My softest verse, my darling lyre,
   Upon Euphelia's toilet lay ;
When Cloe noted her desire,
   That I should sing, that I should play.

My lyre I tune, my voice I raise,
  But with my numbers mix my sighs;
And whilst I sing Euphelia's praise,
  I fix my soul on Cloe's eyes.

Fair Cloe blushed : Euphelia frowned :
  I sung and gazed : I played and trembled :
And Venus to the Loves around
  Remarked, how ill we all dissembled.

AMBROSE PHILLIPS,
1671—1749.

CXVIII.

THE STRAY NYMPH.

CEASE your music, gentle swains :
   Saw ye Delia cross the plains ?
Every thicket, every grove,
Have I ranged, to find my love :
A kid, a lamb, my flock, I give,
Tell me only doth she live.

   White her skin as mountain-snow ;
In her cheek the roses blow ;
And her eye is brighter far
Than the beamy morning star.
When her ruddy lip ye view,
'Tis a berry moist with dew :
And her breath, Oh ! 'tis a gale
Passing o'er a fragrant vale,
Passing, when a friendly shower
Freshens every herb and flower.
Wide her bosom opens, gay
As the primrose-dell in May,
Sweet as violet-borders growing

Over fountains ever-flowing.
Like the tendrils of the vine
Do her auburn tresses twine,
Glossy ringlets all behind
Streaming buxom to the wind,
When along the lawn she bounds,
Light, as hind before the hounds:
And the youthful ring she fires,
Hopeless in their fond desires,
As her flitting feet advance,
Wanton in the winding dance.

Tell me, shepherds, have ye seen
My delight, my love, my queen?

13

CXIX.   THOMAS PARNELL,
                                        1679—1718.

SONG.

M Y days have been so wond'rous free,
    The little birds that fly
With careless ease from tree to tree,
    Were but as blest as I.

Ask gliding waters, if a tear
    Of mine increased their stream?
Or ask the flying gales, if e'er
    I lent one sigh to them?

But now my former days retire,
    And I'm by beauty caught,
The tender chains of sweet desire
    Are fixed upon my thought.

Ye nightingales, ye twisting pines!
    Ye swains that haunt the grove!
Ye gentle echoes, breezy winds!
    Ye close retreats of love!

With all of nature, all of art,
  Assist the dear design ;
O teach a young, unpractised heart,
  To make my Nancy mine.

The very thought of change I hate,
  As much as of despair ;
Nor ever covet to be great,
  Unless it be for her.

'Tis true, the passion in my mind
  Is mixed with soft distress ;
Yet while the fair I love is kind,
  I cannot wish it less.

CXX.   JOHN GAY,
                              1688—1732.

POLYPHEME'S SONG.

O RUDDIER than the cherry !
    O sweeter than the berry !
O nymph more bright
Than moonshine night,
Like kidlings, blithe and merry !
Ripe as the melting cluster,
No lily has such lustre ;
    Yet hard to tame
    As raging flame,
And fierce as storms that bluster.

CXXI.

ALEXANDER POPE,
1688—1744.

ODE ON SOLITUDE.

HAPPY the man whose wish and care
    A few paternal acres bound,
Content to breathe his native air
        In his own ground:

Whose herds with milk, whose fields with bread,
    Whose flocks supply him with attire;
Whose trees in summer yield him shade,
        In winter fire:

Blest, who can unconcernedly find
    Hours, days and years slide soft away;
In health of body, peace of mind,
        Quiet by day:

Sound sleep by night, study and ease,
    Together mixed; sweet recreation;
And innocence, which most does please,
        With meditation.

Thus let me live, unseen, unknown,
      Thus, unlamented, let me die,
Steal from the world, and not a stone
      Tell where I lie.

CXXII.

THE DYING CHRISTIAN TO HIS SOUL.

VITAL spark of heavenly flame !
      Quit, oh ! quit this mortal frame :
Trembling, hoping, lingering, flying,
Oh ! the pain, the bliss of dying.
Cease, fond Nature, cease thy strife,
And let me languish into life.

Hark ! they whisper ; angels say,
'Sister spirit, come away !'
What is this absorbs me quite ?
Steals my senses, shuts my sight,
Drowns my spirit, draws my breath ?
Tell me, my soul, can this be death ?

The world recedes ; it disappears !
Heaven opens on my eyes ! my ears
      With sounds seraphic ring :
Lend, lend your wings ! I mount ! I fly !
O Grave ! where is thy Victory ?
      O Death ! where is thy Sting ?

CXXIII.   HENRY CAREY,
                                       1693?—1743.

SALLY IN OUR ALLEY.

OF all the girls that are so smart
      There's none like pretty Sally ;
She is the darling of my heart,
   And she lives in our alley.
There is no lady in the land
   Is half so sweet as Sally ;
She is the darling of my heart,
   And she lives in our alley.

Her father he makes cabbage-nets,
   And through the streets does cry 'em ;
Her mother she sells laces long
   To such as please to buy 'em :
But sure such folks could ne'er beget
   So sweet a girl as Sally !
She is the darling of my heart,
   And she lives in our alley.

When she is by, I leave my work,
   I love her so sincerely ;

My master comes like any Turk,
  And bangs me most severely :
But let him bang his belly-full,
  I'll bear it all for Sally ;
She is the darling of my heart,
  And she lives in our alley.

Of all the days that's in the week
  I dearly love but one day,
And that's the day that comes betwixt
  A Saturday and Monday;
For then I'm dressed all in my best
  To walk abroad with Sally ;
She is the darling of my heart,
  And she lives in our alley.

My master carries me to church,
  And often am I blamed
Because I leave him in the lurch
  As soon as text is named ;
I leave the church in sermon-time,
  And slink away to Sally ;
She is the darling of my heart,
  And she lives in our alley.

When Christmas comes about again,
  Oh then I shall have money ;

I'll hoard it up and box it all,
   I'll give it to my honey:
I would it were ten thousand pounds,
   I'd give it all to Sally;
She is the darling of my heart,
   And she lives in our alley.

My master and the neighbours all
   Make game of me and Sally;
And, but for her, I'd better be
   A slave and row a galley;
But when my seven long years are out,
   Oh then I'll marry Sally;
Oh then we'll wed, and then we'll bed,
   But not in our alley.

SAMUEL JOHNSON,
1709—1784.

CXXIV.

ON THE DEATH OF MR. ROBERT LEVETT.

CONDEMNED to hope's delusive mine,
   As on we toil from day to day,
By sudden blasts, or slow decline,
   Our social comforts drop away.

Well tried through many a varying year,
   See Levett to the grave descend,
Officious, innocent, sincere,
   Of every friendless name the friend.

Yet still he fills affection's eye,
   Obscurely wise and coarsely kind ;
Nor lettered arrogance deny
   Thy praise to merit unrefined.

When fainting nature called for aid,
   And hovering death prepared the blow,
His vigorous remedy displayed
   The power of art without the show.

In misery's darkest cavern known,
His useful care was ever nigh,
Where hopeless anguish poured his groan,
And lonely want retired to die.

No summons mocked by chill delay,
No petty gain disdained by pride ;
The modest wants of every day
The toil of every day supplied.

His virtues walked their narrow round,
Nor made a pause, nor left a void ;
And sure the eternal Master found
The single talent well employed.

The busy day, the peaceful night,
Unfelt, uncounted, glided by ;
His frame was firm, his powers were bright,
Though now his eightieth year was nigh.

Then, with no fiery throbbing pain,
No cold gradations of decay,
Death broke at once the vital chain,
And freed his soul the nearest way.

CXXV.
WILLIAM COLLINS,
1721—1759.

ODE.

HOW sleep the brave, who sink to rest
By all their country's wishes blest !
When Spring, with dewy fingers cold,
Returns to deck their hallowed mould,
She there shall dress a sweeter sod
Than Fancy's feet have ever trod.

By fairy hands their knell is rung,
By forms unseen their dirge is sung :
There Honour comes, a pilgrim grey,
To bless the turf that wraps their clay ;
And Freedom shall awhile repair,
To dwell a weeping hermit there !

CXXVI.

ON FIDELE, SUPPOSED TO BE DEAD.

TO fair Fidele's grassy tomb,
Soft maids and village hinds shall bring
Each opening sweet, of earliest bloom,
And rifle all the breathing spring.

No wailing ghost shall dare appear
  To vex with shrieks this quiet grove ;
But shepherd-lads assemble here,
  And melting virgins own their love.

No withered witch shall here be seen,
  No goblins lead their nightly crew ;
The female fays shall haunt the green,
  And dress thy grave with pearly dew.

The red-breast oft at evening hours
  Shall kindly lend his little aid,
With hoary moss, and gathered flowers,
  To deck the ground where thou art laid.

When howling winds, and beating rain
  In tempests shake the sylvan cell,
Or midst the chase, on every plain,
  The tender thought on thee shall dwell.

Each lonely scene shall thee restore ;
  For thee the tear be duly shed :
Beloved till life can charm no more ;
  And mourned till Pity's self be dead.

OLIVER GOLDSMITH,
1728—1774.

CXXVII.

OLIVIA'S SONG.

WHEN lovely woman stoops to folly,
    And finds too late that men betray ;
What charm can soothe her melancholy,
    What art can wash her guilt away ?

The only art her guilt to cover,
    To hide her shame from every eye,
To give repentance to her lover,
    And wring his bosom—is to die.

WILLIAM COWPER,
1731—1800.

CXXVIII.

TO MARY.

THE twentieth year is well nigh past,
  Since first our sky was overcast ;
Ah ! would that this might be the last ;
                    My Mary !

Thy spirits have a fainter flow,
I see thee daily weaker grow ;
'Twas my distress that brought thee low,
                    My Mary !

Thy needles, once a shining store,
For my sake restless heretofore,
Now rust disused, and shine no more,
                    My Mary !

For though thou gladly would'st fulfil
The same kind office for me still,
Thy sight now seconds not thy will,
                    My Mary !

But well thou play'dst the housewife's part,
And all thy threads with magic art
Have wound themselves about this heart,
                    My Mary !

Thy indistinct expressions seem
Like language uttered in a dream ;
Yet me they charm, whate'er the theme,
                    My Mary !

Thy silver locks, once auburn bright,
Are still more lovely in my sight
Than golden beams of orient light,
                    My Mary !

For could I view nor them nor thee,
What sight worth seeing could I see ?
The sun would rise in vain for me,
                    My Mary !

Partakers of thy sad decline,
Thy hands their little force resign ;
Yet gently prest, press gently mine,
                    My Mary !

Such feebleness of limbs thou provest,
That now at every step thou movest
Upheld by two, yet still thou lovest,
                    My Mary !

And still to love, though prest with ill,
In wintry age to feel no chill,
With me is to be lovely still,

My Mary !

But ah ! by constant heed I know,
How oft the sadness that I show,
Transforms thy smiles to looks of woe,

My Mary !

And should my future lot be cast
With much resemblance of the past,
Thy worn-out heart will break at last,

My Mary !

14

Anna Letitia Barbauld,
1743—1825.

CXXIX.

LIFE.

L IFE ! I know not what thou art,
   But know that thou and I must part ;
And when, or how, or where we met,
I own to me's a secret yet.
But this I know, when thou art fled,
Where'er they lay these limbs, this head,
No clod so valueless shall be,
As all that then remains of me.
O whither, whither dost thou fly,
Where bend unseen thy trackless course,
   And in this strange divorce,
Ah tell where I must seek this compound I ?
To the vast ocean of empyreal flame,
   From whence thy essence came,
   Dost thou thy flight pursue, when freed
   From matter's base encumbering weed ?
      Or dost thou, hid from sight,
      Wait, like some spell-bound knight,
Through blank oblivious years the appointed hour,
To break thy trance and reassume thy power ?

Yet canst thou without thought or feeling be?
O say what art thou, when no more thou'rt thee?

Life ! we've been long together,
Through pleasant and through cloudy weather;
 'Tis hard to part when friends are dear;
 Perhaps 'twill cost a sigh, a tear;
 Then steal away, give little warning,
  Choose thine own time;
Say not good night, but in some brighter clime
  Bid me good morning.

CXXX.

CHARLES DIBDIN,
1745—1814.

SONG.

B LOW high, blow low, let tempests tear
  The main-mast by the board;
My heart, with thoughts of thee, my dear,
 And love well stored,
Shall brave all danger, scorn all fear,
 The roaring winds, the raging sea,
   In hopes on shore
   To be once more
Safe moored with thee.

Aloft while mountains high we go,
 The whistling winds that scud along,
And the surge roaring from below,
   Shall my signal be
   To think on thee,
 And this shall be my song :

   Blow high, blow low, let tempests tear
   The main-mast by the board.

And on that night when all the crew
 The memory of their former lives,

O'er flowing cans of flip renew,
  And drink their sweethearts and their wives,
    I'll heave a sigh and think on thee ;
        And, as the ship rolls through the sea,
    The burthen of my song shall be,

      Blow high, blow low, let tempests tear
      The main-mast by the board.

WILLIAM BLAKE,
1757—1827.

CXXXI.

SONG.

HOW sweet I roamed from field to field,
   And tasted all the summer's pride,
Till I the Prince of Love beheld,
   Who in the sunny beams did glide.

He shewed me lilies for my hair,
   And blushing roses for my brow ;
He led me through his gardens fair,
   Where all his golden pleasures grow.

With sweet May dews my wings were wet,
   And Phœbus fired my vocal rage ;
He caught me in his silken net,
   And shut me in his golden cage.

He loves to sit and hear me sing,
   Then, laughing, sports and plays with me ;
Then stretches out my golden wing,
   And mocks my loss of liberty.

CXXXII.

SONG.

M Y silks and fine array,
    My smiles and languished air,
By love are driven away ;
    And mournful lean Despair
Brings me yew to deck my grave :
Such end true lovers have.

His face is fair as heaven
    When springing buds unfold ;
O why to him was 't given,
    Whose heart is wintry cold ?
His breast is Love's all-worshipped tomb,
Where all Love's pilgrims come.

Bring me an axe and spade,
    Bring me a winding-sheet ;
When I my grave have made,
    Let winds and tempests beat :
Then down I'll lie, as cold as clay :
True love doth pass away !

CXXXIII

TO THE MUSES.

WHETHER on Ida's shady brow,
 Or in the chambers of the East,
The chambers of the sun, that now
 From ancient melody have ceased ;

Whether in heaven ye wander fair,
 Or the green corners of the earth,
Or the blue regions of the air
 Where the melodious winds have birth ;

Whether on crystal rocks ye rove,
 Beneath the bosom of the sea,
Wandering in many a coral grove ;
 Fair Nine, forsaking Poetry ;

How have you left the ancient love
 That bards of old enjoyed in you !
The languid strings do scarcely move,
 The sound is forced, the notes are few.

CXXXIV.

PIPING down the valleys wild,
    Piping songs of pleasant glee,
On a cloud I saw a child,
    And he laughing said to me :

' Pipe a song about a lamb ! '
    So I piped with merry cheer.
' Piper, pipe that song again ; '
    So I piped : he wept to hear.

' Drop thy pipe, thy happy pipe ;
    Sing thy songs of happy cheer ! '
So I sang the same again,
    While he wept with joy to hear.

' Piper, sit thee down and write
    In a book that all may read ;—'
So he vanished from my sight ;
    And I plucked a hollow reed,

And I made a rural pen,
    And I stained the water clear,
And I wrote my happy songs
    Every child may joy to hear.

CXXXV.

THE TIGER.

TIGER, tiger, burning bright
  In the forest of the night,
What immortal hand or eye
Framed thy fearful symmetry?

In what distant deeps or skies
Burned that fire within thine eyes?
On what wings dared he aspire?
What the hand dared seize the fire?

And what shoulder, and what art,
Could twist the sinews of thy heart?
When thy heart began to beat,
What dread hand formed thy dread feet?

What the hammer, what the chain,
Knit thy strength and forged thy brain?
What the anvil? What dread grasp
Dared thy deadly terrors clasp?

When the stars threw down their spears,
And watered heaven with their tears,
Did he smile his work to see?
Did he who made the lamb make thee?

CXXXVI.   WILLIAM WORDSWORTH,
                             1770—1850.

SHE dwelt among the untrodden ways
   Beside the springs of Dove,
A maid whom there were none to praise,
   And very few to love :

A violet by a mossy stone
   Half hidden from the eye !
Fair as a star, when only one
   Is shining in the sky.

She lived unknown, and few could know
   When Lucy ceased to be ;
But she is in her grave, and, oh !
   The difference to me.

CXXXVII.

TO THE CUCKOO.

O BLITHE new-comer ! I have heard,
   I hear thee, and rejoice.
O Cuckoo ! shall I call thee bird,
Or but a wandering voice ?

While I am lying on the grass
Thy two-fold shout I hear,
From hill to hill it seems to pass,
At once far off and near.

Though babbling only to the vale,
Of sunshine and of flowers,
Thou bringest unto me a tale   ·
Of visionary hours.

Thrice welcome, darling of the spring !
Even yet thou art to me
No bird, but an invisible thing,
A voice, a mystery ;

The same whom in my school-boy days
I listened to ; that cry
Which made me look a thousand ways
In bush, and tree, and sky.

To seek thee did I often rove
Through woods and on the green ;
And thou wert still a hope, a love ;
Still longed for, never seen.

And I can listen to thee yet ;
Can lie upon the plain

And listen, till I do beget
That golden time again.

O blessed bird ! the earth we pace
Again appears to be
An unsubstantial faery place ;
That is fit home for thee !

CXXXVIII.

SHE was a phantom of delight
When first she gleamed upon my sight ;
A lovely apparition, sent
To be a moment's ornament :
Her eyes as stars of twilight fair ;
Like twilight's too her dusky hair ;
But all things else about her drawn
From May-time and the cheerful dawn ;
A dancing shape, an image gay,
To haunt, to startle, and way-lay.

I saw her upon nearer view,
A spirit, yet a woman too !
Her household motions light and free,
And steps of virgin-liberty ;

A countenance in which did meet
Sweet records, promises as sweet ;
A creature not too bright or good
For human nature's daily food ;
For transient sorrows, simple wiles,
Praise, blame, love, kisses, tears, and smiles.

And now I see with eye serene
The very pulse of the machine ;
A being breathing thoughtful breath,
A traveller between life and death ;
The reason firm, the temperate will,
Endurance, foresight, strength, and skill ;
A perfect woman, nobly planned,
To warn, to comfort, and command ;
And yet a spirit still, and bright
With something of angelic light.

CXXXIX.

A SLUMBER did my spirit seal ;
   I had no human fears:
She seemed a thing that could not feel
   The touch of earthly years.

No motion has she now, no force ;
  She neither hears nor sees ;
Rolled round in earth's diurnal course,
  With rocks, and stones, and trees.

CXL.

I WANDERED lonely as a cloud
    That floats on high o'er vales and hills,
When all at once I saw a crowd,
A host, of golden daffodils ;
Beside the lake, beneath the trees,
Fluttering and dancing in the breeze.

Continuous as the stars that shine
And twinkle on the milky way,
They stretched in never-ending line
Along the margin of a bay :
Ten thousand saw I at a glance,
Tossing their heads in sprightly dance.

The waves beside them danced, but they
Outdid the sparkling waves in glee:
A poet could not but be gay,
In such a jocund company:
I gazed—and gazed—but little thought
What wealth the show to me had brought.

For oft, when on my couch I lie
In vacant or in pensive mood,
They flash upon that inward eye
Which is the bliss of solitude ;
And then my heart with pleasure fills,
And dances with the daffodils.

CXLI.

THE SOLITARY REAPER.

BEHOLD her single in the field,
Yon solitary Highland lass !
Reaping and singing by herself ;
Stop here, or gently pass !
Alone she cuts and binds the grain,
And sings a melancholy strain ;
Oh listen ! for the vale profound
Is overflowing with the sound.

No nightingale did ever chaunt
More welcome notes to weary bands
Of travellers in some shady haunt
Among Arabian sands ;
A voice so thrilling ne'er was heard
In spring time from the cuckoo-bird,
Breaking the silence of the seas
Among the farthest Hebrides.

15

Will no one tell me what she sings?
Perhaps the plaintive numbers flow
For old, unhappy, far-off things,
And battles long ago:
Or is it some more humble lay,
Familiar matter of to-day?
Some natural sorrow, loss, or pain,
That has been, and may be again !

Whate'er the theme, the maiden sang
As if her song could have no ending,
I saw her singing at her work,
And o'er the sickle bending ;—
I listened, motionless and still ;
And, as I mounted up the hill,
The music in my heart I bore,
Long after it was heard no more.

°

Sir Walter Scott,
1771—1832.

CXLII.

FITZ-EUSTACE'S SONG.

WHERE shall the lover rest,
  Whom the fates sever
From his true maiden's breast
  Parted for ever?
Where, through groves deep and high,
  Sounds the far billow,
Where early violets die,
  Under the willow.

There, through the summer day,
  Cool streams are laving ;
There while the tempests sway,
  Scarce are boughs waving ;
There, thy rest shalt thou take,
  Parted for ever,
Never again to wake,
  Never, oh never !

Where shall the traitor rest,
  He, the deceiver,

Who could win maiden's breast,
  Ruin, and leave her ?
In the lost battle
  Borne down by the flying,
Where mingles war's rattle
  With groans of the dying.

Her wing shall the eagle flap
  O'er the false-hearted ;
His warm blood the wolf shall lap,
  Ere life be parted,
Shame and dishonour sit
  By his grave ever ;
Blessing shall hallow it,—
  Never, oh never.

CXLIII.

SONG.

A WEARY lot is thine, fair maid,
    A weary lot is thine !
To pull the thorn thy brow to braid,
  And press the rue for wine !
A lightsome eye, a soldier's mien,
  A feather of the blue,
A doublet of the Lincoln green,—

No more of me you knew,
                My love !
No more of me you knew.

This morn is merry June, I trow,
   The rose is budding fain ;
But she shall bloom in winter snow,
   Ere we two meet again.
He turned his charger as he spake,
   Upon the river shore,
He gave his bridle-reins a shake,
   Said, 'Adieu for evermore,
                My love !
And adieu for evermore.'

CXLIV.

LUCY ASHTON'S SONG.

LOOK not thou on beauty's charming,—
   Sit thou still when kings are arming,—
Taste not when the wine-cup glistens,—
Speak not when the people listens,—
Stop thine ear against the singer,—
From the red gold keep thy finger,—
Vacant heart, and hand, and eye,
Easy live and quiet die.

CXLV.

SONG.

AH ! County Guy, the hour is nigh,
　　The sun has left the lea,
The orange-flower perfumes the bower,
　　The breeze is on the sea.
The lark, his lay who trilled all day,
　　Sits hushed his partner nigh ;
Breeze, bird, and flower confess the hour,
　　But where is County Guy ?

The village maid steals through the shade
　　Her shepherd's suit to hear ;
To beauty shy, by lattice high,
　　Sings high-born cavalier.
The star of love, all stars above,
　　Now reigns o'er earth and sky ;
And high and low the influence know—
　　But where is County Guy ?

CXLVI

FLORA'S SONG.

THE sun upon the lake is low,
    The wild birds hush their song,
The hills have evening's deepest glow,
    Yet Leonard tarries long.
Now all whom varied toil and care
    From home and love divide,
In the calm sunset may repair
    Each to the loved one's side.

The noble dame on turret high,
    Who waits her gallant knight,
Looks to the western beam to spy
    The flash of armour bright.
The village maid, with hand on brow,
    The level ray to shade,
Upon the footpath watches now
    For Colin's darkening plaid.

Now to their mates the wild swans row,
    By day they swam apart,
And to the thicket wanders slow
    The hind beside the hart.

The woodlark at his partner's side
Twitters his closing song—
All meet whom day and care divide,
But Leonard tarries long !

CXLVII.

SAMUEL TAYLOR COLERIDGE,
1772—1834.

THE KNIGHT'S TOMB.

WHERE is the grave of Sir Arthur O'Kellyn?
　　Where may the grave of that good man be?—
By the side of a spring, on the breast of Helvellyn,
Under the twigs of a young birch tree!
The oak that in summer was sweet to hear,
And rustled its leaves in the fall of the year,
And whistled and roared in the winter alone,
Is gone, and the birch in its stead is grown.
The Knight's bones are dust,
And his good sword rust;—
His soul is with the saints, I trust.

CXLVIII.

YOUTH AND AGE.

VERSE, a breeze 'mid blossoms straying,
　　Where Hope clung feeding, like a bee—
Both were mine! life went a-maying
　　With Nature, Hope, and Poesy,
　　　When I was young!

When I was young? ah! woeful when;
Ah! for the change 'twixt now and then;
This breathing house not built with hands,
This body that does me grievous wrong,
O'er aery cliffs and glittering sands,
How lightly then it flashed along:
Like those trim skiffs, unknown of yore,
On winding lakes and rivers wide,
That ask no aid of sail or oar,
That fear no spite of wind or tide!
Nought cared this body for wind or weather
When youth and I lived in 't together.

Flowers are lovely; love is flower-like;
Friendship is a sheltering tree;
O! the joys, that came down shower-like,
Of Friendship, Love, and Liberty,
                    Ere I was old!
Ere I was old? Ah woeful ere!
Which tells me, youth's no longer here.
O youth! for years so many and sweet,
'Tis known, that thou and I were one,
I'll think it but a fond conceit—
It cannot be that thou art gone!
Thy vesper-bell hath not yet tolled:
And thou wert aye a masker bold!
What strange disguise hast now put on,

To make believe; that thou art gone?
I see these locks in silvery slips,
This drooping gait, this altered size :
But spring-tide blossoms on thy lips,
And tears take sunshine from thine eyes !
Life is but thought: so think I will
That youth and I are house-mates still.

CXLIX.

GLYCINE'S SONG.

A SUNNY shaft did I behold,
   From sky to earth it slanted;
And poised therein a bird so bold—
   Sweet bird, thou wert enchanted !

He sank, he rose, he twinkled, he trolled
   Within that shaft of sunny mist ;
His eyes of fire, his beak of gold,
   All else of amethyst !

And thus he sang: 'Adieu ! adieu !
   Love's dreams prove seldom true.
     The blossoms they
      Make no delay ;

The sparkling dewdrops will not stay.
Sweet month of May,
We must away ;
Far, far away !
To-day ! to-day !'

CL.   ROBERT SOUTHEY,
                                        1774—1843.

THE HOLLY TREE.

O READER ! hast thou ever stood to see
        The holly tree ?
The eye that contemplates it well perceives
        Its glossy leaves
Ordered by an intelligence so wise,
As might confound the atheist's sophistries.

Below, a circling fence, its leaves are seen
        Wrinkled and keen ;
No grazing cattle through their prickly round
        Can reach to wound ;
But as they grow where nothing is to fear,
Smooth and unarmed the pointless leaves appear.

I love to view these things with curious eyes,
        And moralize :
And in this wisdom of the holly tree
        Can emblems see
Wherewith perchance to make a pleasant rhyme,
One which may profit in the after time.

Thus, though abroad perchance I might appear
    Harsh and austere,
To those who on my leisure would intrude
    Reserved and rude,
Gentle at home amid my friends I'd be
Like the high leaves upon the holly tree.

And should my youth, as youth is apt I know,
    Some harshness show,
All vain asperities I day by day
    Would wear away,
Till the smooth temper of my age should be
Like the high leaves upon the holly tree.

And as when all the summer trees are seen
    So bright and green,
The holly leaves a sober hue display
    Less bright than they,
But when the bare and wintry woods we see,
What then so cheerful as the holly tree?

So serious should my youth appear among
    The thoughtless throng,
So would I seem amid the young and gay
    More grave than they,
That in my age as cheerful I might be
As the green winter of the holly tree.

CLI.

CHARLES LAMB,
1775—1834.

HESTER.

WHEN maidens such as Hester die,
    Their place ye may not well supply,
Though ye among a thousand try,
      With vain endeavour.

A month or more hath she been dead,
Yet cannot I by force be led
To think upon the wormy bed,
      And her together.

A springy motion in her gait,
A rising step, did indicate
Of pride and joy no common rate,
      That flushed her spirit.

I know not by what name beside
I shall it call: if 'twas not pride,
It was a joy to that allied,
      She did inherit.

Her parents held the Quaker rule,
Which doth the human feeling cool,
But she was trained in Nature's school,
    Nature had blest her.

A waking eye, a prying mind,
A heart that stirs, is hard to bind,
A hawk's keen sight ye cannot blind,
    Ye could not Hester.

My sprightly neighbour, gone before
To that unknown and silent shore,
Shall we not meet, as heretofore,
    Some summer morning,

When from thy cheerful eyes a ray
Hath struck a bliss upon the day,
A bliss that would not go away,
    A sweet fore-warning?

CLII.

THE OLD FAMILIAR FACES.

I HAVE had playmates, I have had companions,
  In my days of childhood, in my joyful school-days,
All, all are gone, the old familiar faces.

I have been laughing, I have been carousing,
Drinking late, sitting late, with my bosom cronies,
All, all are gone, the old familiar faces.

I loved a love once, fairest among women ;
Closed are her doors on me, I must not see her—
All, all are gone, the old familiar faces.

I have a friend, a kinder friend has no man ;
Like an ingrate, I left my friend abruptly ;
Left him, to muse on the old familiar faces.

Ghost-like I paced round the haunts of my childhood.
Earth seemed a desert I was bound to traverse,
Seeking to find the old familiar faces.

Friend of my bosom, thou more than a brother,
Why wert not thou born in my father's dwelling?
So might we talk of the old familiar faces—

How some they have died, and some they have left me,
And some are taken from me ; all are departed ;
All, all are gone, the old familiar faces.

16

Thomas Campbell,
1777—1844.

CLIII.

YE MARINERS OF ENGLAND.

A NAVAL ODE.

YE mariners of England!
  That guard our native seas;
Whose flag has braved a thousand years,
The battle and the breeze!
Your glorious standard launch again
To match another foe!
And sweep through the deep,
While the stormy winds do blow;
While the battle rages loud and long,
And the stormy winds do blow.

The spirits of your fathers
Shall start from every wave!
For the deck it was their field of fame,
And ocean was their grave:
Where Blake and mighty Nelson fell
Your manly hearts shall glow,
As ye sweep through the deep,
While the stormy winds do blow;

While the battle rages loud and long,
And the stormy winds do blow.

Britannia needs no bulwark,
No towers along the steep;
Her march is o'er the mountain waves,
Her home is on the deep.
With thunders from her native oak,
She quells the floods below,—
As they roar on the shore,
When the stormy winds do blow;
When the battle rages loud and long,
And the stormy winds do blow.

The meteor flag of England
Shall yet terrific burn;
Till danger's troubled night depart,
And the star of peace return.
Then, then, ye ocean warriors!
Our song and feast shall flow
To the fame of your name,
When the storm has ceased to blow;
When the fiery fight is heard no more,
And the storm has ceased to blow.

CLIV.

HOHENLINDEN.

ON Linden, when the sun was low,
All bloodless lay the untrodden snow,
And dark as winter was the flow
Of Iser, rolling rapidly.

But Linden saw another sight,
When the drum beat, at dead of night,
Commanding fires of death to light
The darkness of her scenery.

By torch and trumpet fast arrayed
Each horseman drew his battle-blade,
And furious every charger neighed
To join the dreadful revelry.

Then shook the hills with thunder riven,
Then rushed the steed to battle driven,
And louder than the bolts of heaven,
Far flashed the red artillery.

But redder yet that light shall glow
On Linden's hills of stained snow,
And bloodier yet the torrent flow
Of Iser, rolling rapidly.

'Tis morn, but scarce yon level sun
Can pierce the war-clouds, rolling dun,
Where furious Frank, and fiery Hun
Shout in their sulph'rous canopy.

The combat deepens.   On, ye brave,
Who rush to glory, or the grave !
Wave, Munich ! all thy banners wave,
And charge with all thy chivalry !

Few, few, shall part where many meet !
The snow shall be their winding-sheet,
And every turf beneath their feet
Shall be a soldier's sepulchre.

CLV.

SONG.

HOW delicious is the winning
   Of a kiss at love's beginning,
When two mutual hearts are sighing
For the knot there's no untying !

Yet remember, 'midst your wooing,
Love has bliss, but love has rueing ;

Other smiles may make you fickle,
Tears for other charms may trickle.

Love he comes, and love he tarries,
Just as fate or fancy carries ;
Longest stays, when sorest chidden ;
Laughs and flies, when pressed and bidden.

Bind the sea to slumber stilly,
Bind its odour to the lily,
Bind the aspen ne'er to quiver,
Then bind love to last for ever !

Love's a fire that needs renewal
Of fresh beauty for its fuel ;
Love's wing moults when caged and captured,
Only free he soars enraptured.

Can you keep the bee from ranging,
Or the ringdove's neck from changing?
No ! nor fettered love from dying,
In the knot there's no untying.

CLVI.

MARGARET AND DORA.

M ARGARET 'S beauteous—Grecian arts
    Ne'er drew form completer ;
Yet why, in my heart of hearts,
Hold I Dora 's sweeter?

Dora's eyes of heavenly blue
Pass all painting's reach,
Ringdoves' notes are discord to
The music of her speech.

Artists ! Margaret's smile receive,
And on canvas show it ;
But for perfect worship leave
Dora to her poet.

CLVII.

Ebenezer Elliott,
1781—1849.

PLAINT.

DARK, deep, and cold the current flows
  Unto the sea where no wind blows,
Seeking the land which no one knows.

O'er its sad gloom still comes and goes
The mingled wail of friends and foes,
Borne to the land which no one knows.

Why shrieks for help yon wretch, who goes
With millions, from a world of woes,
Unto the land which no one knows?

Though myriads go with him who goes,
Alone he goes where no wind blows,
Unto the land which no one knows.

For all must go where no wind blows,
And none can go for him who goes;
None, none return whence no one knows.

Yet why should he who shrieking goes
With millions, from a world of woes,
Reunion seek with it or those ?

Alone with God, where no wind blows,
And Death, his shadow—doomed, he goes :
That God is there the shadow shows.

Oh shoreless Deep, where no wind blows !
And, thou, oh Land, which no one knows !
That God is All, his shadow shows.

CLVIII.

THOMAS LOVE PEACOCK,
1785—1866.

THE FRIAR'S SONG.

THOUGH I be now a gray, gray friar,
    Yet I was once a hale young knight:
The cry of my dogs was the only choir
    In which my spirit did take delight.

Little I recked of matin bell,
    But drowned its toll with my clanging horn:
And the only beads I loved to tell
    Were the beads of dew on the spangled thorn.

An archer keen I was withal,
    As ever did lean on greenwood tree;
And could make the fleetest roebuck fall,
    A good three hundred yards from me.

Though changeful time, with hand severe,
    Has made me now these joys forego,
Yet my heart bounds whene'er I hear
    Yoicks ! hark away ! and tally ho

CLIX.

THE WAR-SONG OF DINAS VAWR.

THE mountain sheep are sweeter,
   But the valley sheep are fatter ;
We therefore deemed it meeter
To carry off the latter.
We made an expedition ;
We met an host and quelled it ;
We forced a strong position,
And killed the men who held it.

On Dyfed's richest valley,
Where herds of kine were browsing,
We made a mighty sally,
To furnish our carousing.
Fierce warriors rushed to meet us ;
We met them, and o'erthrew them :
They struggled hard to beat us,
But we conquered them, and slew them.

As we drove our prize at leisure,
The king marched forth to catch us :
His rage surpassed all measure,
But his people could not match us.

He fled to his hall-pillars ;
And, ere our force we led off,
Some sacked his house and cellars,
While others cut his head off.

We there, in strife bewildering,
Spilt blood enough to swim in :
We orphaned many children,
And widowed many women.
The eagles and the ravens
We glutted with our foemen ;
The heroes and the cravens,
The spearmen and the bowmen.

We brought away from battle,
And much their land bemoaned them,
Two thousand head of cattle,
And the head of him who owned them :
Ednyfed, King of Dyfed,
His head was borne before us ;
His wine and beasts supplied our feasts,
And his overthrow, our chorus.

CLX.

BEYOND the sea, beyond the sea,
My heart is gone, far, far from me ;
And ever on its track will flee
My thoughts, my dreams, beyond the sea.

Beyond the sea, beyond the sea,
The swallow wanders fast and free :
Oh ! happy bird, were I like thee,
I, too, would fly beyond the sea.

Beyond the sea, beyond the sea,
Are kindly hearts and social glee :
But here for me they may not be :
My heart is gone beyond the sea.

CLXI.

LADY CLARINDA'S SONG.

IN the days of old,
Lovers felt true passion,
Deeming years of sorrow
By a smile repaid.

Now the charms of gold,
Spells of pride and fashion,
Bid them say good morrow
To the best-loved maid.

Through the forests wild,
O'er the mountains lonely,
They were never weary
Honour to pursue:
If the damsel smiled
Once in seven years only,
All their wanderings dreary
Ample guerdon knew.

Now one day's caprice
Weighs down years of smiling,
Youthful hearts are rovers,
Love is bought and sold:
Fortune's gifts may cease,
Love is less beguiling ;
Wiser were the lovers,
In the days of old.

CLXII.

LOVE AND AGE.

I PLAYED with you 'mid cowslips blowing,
   When I was six and you were four ;
When garlands weaving, flower-balls throwing,
   Were pleasures soon to please no more.
Through groves and meads, o'er grass and heather,
   With little playmates, to and fro,
We wandered hand in hand together ;—
   But that was sixty years ago.

You grew a lovely roseate maiden,
   And still our early love was strong ;
Still with no care our days were laden,
   They glided joyously along ;
And I did love you very dearly,
   How dearly words want power to show ;
I thought your heart was touched as nearly ;—
   But that was fifty years ago.

Then other lovers came around you,
   Your beauty grew from year to year,
And many a splendid circle found you
   The centre of its glittering sphere.

I saw you then, first vows forsaking,
On rank and wealth your hand bestow ;
Oh ! then I thought my heart was breaking ;—
But that was forty years ago.

And I lived on, to wed another :
No cause she gave me to repine ;
And when I heard you were a mother,
I did not wish the children mine.
My own young flock, in fair progression,
Made up a pleasant Christmas row :
My joy in them was past expression,—
But that was thirty years ago.

You grew a matron plump and comely,
You dwelt in fashion's brightest blaze ;
My earthly lot was far more homely ;
But I too had my festal days.
No merrier eyes have ever glistened
Around the hearth-stone's wintry glow,
Than when my youngest child was christened,—
But that was twenty years ago.

Time passed.   My eldest girl was married,
And I am now a grandsire gray ;
One pet of four years old I've carried
Among the wild-flowered meads to play.

In our old fields of childish pleasure,
Where now, as then, the cowslips blow,
She fills her basket's ample measure,—
And that is not ten years ago.

But though first love's impassioned blindness
Has passed away in colder light,
I still have thought of you with kindness,
And shall do, till our last good-night.
The ever-rolling silent hours
Will bring a time we shall not know,
When our young days of gathering flowers
Will be an hundred years ago.

17

CLXIII.   GEORGE GORDON, LORD BYRON,
                                              1788—1824

SHE walks in beauty, like the night
    Of cloudless climes and starry skies;
And all that's best of dark and bright
    Meet in her aspect and her eyes:
Thus mellowed to that tender light
    Which heaven to gaudy day denies.

One shade the more, one ray the less,
    Had half impaired the nameless grace
Which waves in every raven tress,
    Or softly lightens o'er her face;
Where thoughts serenely sweet express,
    How pure, how dear their dwelling-place.

And on that cheek, and o'er that brow,
    So soft, so calm, yet eloquent,
The smiles that win, the tints that glow,
    But tell of days in goodness spent,
A mind at peace with all below,
    A heart whose love is innocent.

CLXIV.

BRIGHT be the place of thy soul !
   No lovelier spirit than thine
E'er burst from its mortal control,
   In the orbs of the blessed to shine.
On earth thou wert all but divine,
   As thy soul shall immortally be ;
And our sorrow may cease to repine
   When we know that thy God is with thee.

Light be the turf of thy tomb !
   May its verdure like emeralds be !
There should not be the shadow of gloom,
   In aught that reminds us of thee.
Young flowers and an evergreen tree
   May spring from the spot of thy rest :
But nor cypress nor yew let us see ;
   For why should we mourn for the blest ?

CLXV.

WHEN we two parted
        In silence and tears,
Half broken-hearted,
    To sever for years ;
Pale grew thy cheek and cold,
    Colder thy kiss ;
Truly that hour foretold
    Sorrow to this.

The dew of the morning
    Sunk chill on my brow—
It felt like the warning
    Of what I feel now.
Thy vows are all broken,
    And light is thy fame ;
I hear thy name spoken
    And share in its shame.

They name thee before me,
    A knell to mine ear ;
A shudder comes o'er me—
    Why wert thou so dear ?

They know not I knew thee,
    Who knew thee too well :—
Long, long shall I rue thee,
    Too deeply to tell.

In secret we met—
    In silence I grieve,
That thy heart could forget,
    Thy spirit deceive.
If I should meet thee
    After long years,
How should I greet thee ?—
    With silence and tears.

CLXVI.

STANZAS FOR MUSIC.

THERE be none of Beauty's daughters
    With a magic like thee ;
And like music on the waters
    Is thy sweet voice to me :
When, as if its sound were causing
The charmed ocean's pausing,
The waves lie still and gleaming
And the lulled winds seem dreaming.

And the midnight moon is weaving
  Her bright chain o'er the deep ;
Whose breast is gently heaving,
  As an infant's asleep :
So the spirit bows before thee,
To listen and adore thee ;
With a full but soft emotion,
Like the swell of summer's ocean.

CLXVII.

OH ! snatched away in beauty's bloom,
  On thee shall press no ponderous tomb ;
But on thy turf shall roses rear
Their leaves, the earliest of the year ;
And the wild cypress wave in tender gloom :

And oft by yon blue gushing stream
  Shall Sorrow lean her drooping head,
And feed deep thought with many a dream,
  And lingering pause and lightly tread ;
  Fond wretch ! as if her step disturbed the dead !

Away ! we know that tears are vain,
   That death nor heeds nor hears distress :
Will this unteach us to complain?
   Or make one mourner weep the less?
And thou—who tell'st me to forget,
Thy looks are wan, thine eyes are wet.

CLXVIII.

CHARLES WOLFE,
1791—1823.

SONG.

IF I had thought thou could'st have died,
    I might not weep for thee ;
But I forgot, when by thy side,
    That thou could'st mortal be ;
It never through my mind had past,
    The time would e'er be o'er,
And I on thee should look my last,
    And thou should'st smile no more !

And still upon that face I look,
    And think 'twill smile again ;
And still the thought I will not brook,
    That I must look in vain !
But when I speak—thou dost not say,
    What thou ne'er left'st unsaid,
And now I feel, as well I may,
    Sweet Mary ! thou art dead !

If thou would'st stay, e'en as thou art,
    All cold, and all serene—

I still might press thy silent heart,
  And where thy smiles have been !
While e'en thy chill bleak corse I have,
  Thou seemest still mine own ;
But there I lay thee in thy grave—
  And I am now alone !

I do not think, where'er thou art,
  Thou hast forgotten me ;
And I, perhaps, may soothe this heart,
  In thinking too of thee ;
Yet there was round thee such a dawn
  Of light ne'er seen before,
As fancy never could have drawn,
  And never can restore !

CLXIX.

THE BURIAL OF SIR JOHN MOORE.

NOT a drum was heard, not a funeral note,
  As his corse to the rampart we hurried ;
Not a soldier discharged his farewell shot
  O'er the grave where our hero we buried.

We buried him darkly at dead of night,
  The sods with our bayonets turning ;

By the struggling moonbeam's misty light,
  And the lantern dimly burning.

No useless coffin enclosed his breast,
  Not in sheet or in shroud we wound him ;
But he lay like a warrior taking his rest,
  With his martial cloak around him.

Few and short were the prayers we said,
  And we spoke not a word of sorrow ;
But we steadfastly gazed on the face that was dead,
  And we bitterly thought of the morrow.

We thought, as we hollowed his narrow bed,
  And smoothed down his lonely pillow,
That the foe and the stranger would tread o'er his head,
  And we far away on the billow !

Lightly they'll talk of the spirit that's gone,
  And o'er his cold ashes upbraid him,—
But little he'll reck, if they let him sleep on
  In the grave where a Briton has laid him.

But half of our heavy task was done,
  When the clock struck the hour for retiring ;
And we heard the distant and random gun
  That the foe was sullenly firing.

CHARLES WOLFE.

Slowly and sadly we laid him down,
   From the field of his fame fresh and gory;
We carved not a line, and we raised not a stone—
   But we left him alone with his glory!

CLXX.

PERCY BYSSHE SHELLEY,
1792—1822.

STANZAS.

APRIL, 1814.

A WAY ! the moor is dark beneath the moon.
    Rapid clouds have drunk the last pale beam of
      even:
Away ! the gathering winds will call the darkness soon,
    And profoundest midnight shroud the serene lights of
      heaven.
Pause not ! The time is past ! Every voice cries, Away !
    Tempt not with one last glance thy friend's ungentle
      mood:
Thy lover's eye, so glazed and cold, dares not entreat thy
      stay:
    Duty and dereliction guide thee back to solitude.

Away, away ! to thy sad and silent home ;
    Pour bitter tears on its desolated hearth ;
Watch the dim shades as like ghosts they go and come,
    And complicate strange webs of melancholy mirth.
The leaves of wasted autumn woods shall float around
      thine head ;
    The blooms of dewy spring shall gleam beneath thy feet:

But thy soul or this world must fade in the frost that binds
    the dead,
  Ere midnight's frown and morning's smile, ere thou and
    peace may meet.

The cloud shadows of midnight possess their own repose,
  For the weary winds are silent, or the moon is in the
    deep ;
Some respite to its turbulence unresting ocean knows ;
  Whatever moves, or toils, or grieves, hath its appointed
    sleep.
Thou in the grave shalt rest—yet till the phantoms flee
  Which that house and heath and garden made dear to
    thee erewhile,
Thy remembrance, and repentance, and deep musings are
    not free
  From the music of two voices and the light of one sweet
    smile.

CLXXI.

STANZAS.

WRITTEN IN DEJECTION, NEAR NAPLES.

THE sun is warm, the sky is clear,
    The waves are dancing fast and bright,
Blue isles and snowy mountains wear
    The purple noon's transparent might :

The breath of the moist earth is light,
　　Around its unexpanded buds ;
Like many a voice of one delight,
　　The winds, the birds, the ocean floods,
The city's voice itself is soft like solitude's.

I see the deep's untrampled floor
　　With green and purple sea-weeds strown ;
I see the waves upon the shore,
　　Like light dissolved in star-showers, thrown :
I sit upon the sands alone,
　　The lightning of the noon-tide ocean
Is flashing round me, and a tone
　　Arises from its measured motion,
How sweet ! did any heart now share in my emotion.

Alas ! I have nor hope nor health,
　　Nor peace within nor calm around,
Nor that content surpassing wealth
　　The sage in meditation found,
And walked with inward glory crowned—
　　Nor fame, nor power, nor love, nor leisure.
Others I see whom these surround—
　　Smiling they live and call life pleasure ;—
To me that cup has been dealt in another measure.

Yet now despair itself is mild,
　　Even as the winds and waters are ;

I could lie down like a tired child,
    And weep away the life of care
Which I have borne and yet must bear,
    Till death like sleep might steal on me,
And I might feel in the warm air
    My cheek grow cold, and hear the sea
Breathe o'er my dying brain its last monotony.

Some might lament that I were cold,
    As I, when this sweet day is gone,
Which my lost heart, too soon grown old,
    Insults with this untimely moan ;
They might lament—for I am one
    Whom men love not—and yet regret,
Unlike this day, which, when the sun
    Shall on its stainless glory set,
Will linger, though enjoyed, like joy in memory yet.

CLXXII.

SONG.

TO THE MEN OF ENGLAND.

MEN of England, wherefore plough
    For the lords who lay ye low ?
Wherefore weave with toil and care
The rich robes your tyrants wear ?

Wherefore feed, and clothe, and save,
From the cradle to the grave,
Those ungrateful drones who would
Drain your sweat—nay, drink your blood?

Wherefore, bees of England, forge
Many a weapon, chain, and scourge,
That these stingless drones may spoil
The forced produce of your toil?

Have ye leisure, comfort, calm,   .
Shelter, food, love's gentle balm?
Or what is it ye buy so dear
With your pain and with your fear?

The seed ye sow, another reaps;
The wealth ye find, another keeps;
The robes ye weave, another wears;
The arms ye forge, another bears.

Sow seed,—but let no tyrant reap;
Find wealth,—let no impostor heap;
Weave robes,—let not the idle wear;
Forge arms,—in your defence to bear.

Shrink to your cellars, holes, and cells;
In halls ye deck another dwells.

Why shake the chains ye wrought ?   Ye see
The steel ye tempered glance on ye.

With plough and spade, and hoe and loom,
Trace your grave, and build your tomb,
And weave your winding-sheet, till fair
England be your sepulchre.

CLXXIIL

TO ——

ONE word is too often profaned
    For me to profane it,
One feeling too falsely disdained
    For thee to disdain it.
One hope is too like despair
    For prudence to smother,   .
And pity from thee more dear
    Than that from another.

I can give not what men call love,
    But wilt thou accept not
The worship the heart lifts above
    And the heavens reject not ;

18

The desire of the moth for the star,
    Of the night for the morrow,
The devotion to something afar
    From the sphere of our sorrow ?

CLXXIV.

LINES.

WHEN the lamp is shattered
    The light in the dust lies dead—
When the cloud is scattered
The rainbow's glory is shed.
    When the lute is broken,
Sweet tones are remembered not ;
    When the lips have spoken,
Loved accents are soon forgot.

    · As music and splendour
Survive not the lamp and the lute,
    The heart's echoes render
No song when the spirit is mute :—
    No song but sad dirges,
Like the wind through a ruined cell,
    Or the mournful surges
That ring the dead seaman's knell.

When hearts have once mingled
Love first leaves the well-built nest,
The weak one is singled
To endure what it once possest.
O Love! who bewailest
The frailty of all things here,
Why choose you the frailest
For your cradle, your home, and your bier?

Its passions will rock thee
As the storms rock the ravens on high:
Bright reason will mock thee,
Like the sun from a wintry sky.
From thy nest every rafter
Will rot, and thine eagle home
Leave thee naked to laughter,
When leaves fall and cold winds come.

CLXXV.

NATIONAL ANTHEM.

GOD prosper, speed, and save,
God raise from England's grave
Her murdered Queen!

Pave with swift victory
The steps of Liberty,
Whom Britons own to be
            Immortal Queen.

See, she comes throned on high,
On swift Eternity !
            God save the Queen !
Millions on millions wait
Firm, rapid, and elate,
On her majestic state !
            God save the Queen !

She is thine own pure soul
Moulding the mighty whole, —
            God save the Queen !
She is thine own deep love
Rained down from heaven above,
Where'er she rest or move, —
            God save our Queen !

Wilder her enemies
In their own dark disguise, —
            God save our Queen !
All earthly things that dare
Her sacred name to bear,
Strip them, as kings are, bare ;
            God save the Queen !

Be her eternal throne
Built in our hearts alone,—
                    God save the Queen !
Let the oppressor hold
Canopied seats of gold ;
She sits enthroned of old
                    O'er our hearts Queen.

Lips touched by seraphim
Breathe out the choral hymn
                    ' God save the Queen !'
Sweet as if angels sang,
Loud as that trumpet's clang
Wakening the world's dead gang,—
                    God save the Queen !

FELICIA HEMANS,
1793—1835.

CLXXVI.

THE TREASURES OF THE DEEP.

WHAT hidest thou in thy treasure-caves and cells ?
    Thou hollow-sounding and mysterious main !—
Pale glistening pearls, and rainbow-coloured shells,
    Bright things which gleam unrecked of and in vain !—
Keep, keep thy riches, melancholy sea !
      We ask not such from thee.

Yet more, the depths have more ! What wealth untold,
    Far down, and shining through their stillness lies !
Thou hast the starry gems, the burning gold,
    Won from ten thousand royal argosies.
Sweep o'er thy spoils, thou wild and wrathful main !
      Earth claims not these again.

Yet more, the depths have more ! Thy waves have rolled
    Above the cities of a world gone by ;
Sand hath filled up the palaces of old,
    Sea-weed o'ergrown the halls of revelry.
Dash o'er them, ocean ! in thy scornful play :
      Man yields them to decay.

Yet more ! the billows and the depths have more !
   High hearts and brave are gathered to thy breast !
They hear not now the booming waters roar,
   The battle-thunders will not break their rest.
Keep thy red gold and gems, thou stormy grave !
      Give back the true and brave !

Give back the lost and lovely ! those for whom
   The place was kept at board and hearth so long !
The prayer went up through midnight's breathless gloom,
   And the vain yearning woke 'midst festal song !
Hold fast thy buried isles, thy towers o'erthrown—
      But all is not thine own.

To thee the love of woman hath gone down,
   Dark flow thy tides o'er manhood's noble head,
O'er youth's bright locks, and beauty's flowery crown ;
   Yet must thou hear a voice—Restore the dead !
Earth shall reclaim her precious things from thee !
      Restore the dead, thou sea !

John Keats,
1795—1821.

CLXXVII.

ROBIN HOOD.

TO A FRIEND.

NO ! those days are gone away,
  And their hours are old and grey,
And their minutes buried all
Under the down-trodden pall
Of the leaves of many years :
Many times have winter's shears,
Frozen north, and chilling east,
Sounded tempests to the feast
Of the forest's whispering fleeces,
Since men knew nor rent nor leases.

  No, the bugle sounds no more,
And the twanging bow no more ;
Silent is the ivory shrill
Past the heath and up the hill ;
There is no mid-forest laugh,
Where lone Echo gives the half
To some wight, amazed to hear
Jesting, deep in forest drear.

On the fairest time of June
You may go, with sun or moon,
Or the seven stars to light you,
Or the polar ray to right you ;
But you never may behold
Little John, or Robin bold ;
Never one, of all the clan,
Thrumming on an empty can
Some old hunting ditty, while
He doth his green way beguile
To fair hostess Merriment,
Down beside the pasture Trent ;
For he left the merry tale,
Messenger for spicy ale.

Gone, the merry morris din ;
Gone, the song of Gamelyn ;
Gone, the tough-belted outlaw
Idling in the ' grené shawe ; '
All are gone away and past !
And if Robin should be cast
Sudden from his tufted grave,
And if Marian should have
Once again her forest days,
She would weep, and he would craze :
He would swear, for all his oaks,
Fall'n beneath the dock-yard strokes,

Have rotted on the briny seas ;
She would weep that her wild bees
Sang not to her—strange ! that honey
Can't be got without hard money !

So it is ; yet let us sing
Honour to the old bow-string !
Honour to the bugle-horn !
Honour to the woods unshorn !
Honour to the Lincoln green !
Honour to the archer keen !
Honour to tight Little John,
And the horse he rode upon !
Honour to bold Robin Hood,
Sleeping in the underwood !
Honour to Maid Marian,
And to all the Sherwood clan !
Though their days have hurried by,
Let us two a burden try.

CLXXVIII.

IN a drear-nighted December,
   Too happy, happy tree,
Thy branches ne'er remember
Their green felicity :

The north cannot undo them
With a sleety whistle through them ;
Nor frozen thawings glue them
From budding at the prime.

In a drear-nighted December,
Too happy, happy brook,
Thy bubblings ne'er remember
Apollo's summer look ;
But with a sweet forgetting,
They stay their crystal fretting,
Never, never petting
About the frozen time.

Ah ! would 'twere so with many
A gentle girl and boy ;
But were there ever any
Writhed not at passed joy ?
To know the change and feel it,
When there is none to heal it,
Nor numbed sense to steal it,
Was never said in rhyme.

CLXXIX.

HARTLEY COLERIDGE,
1796—1849.

SONG.

SHE is not fair to outward view
  As many maidens be,
Her loveliness I never knew
  Until she smiled on me ;
Oh ! then I saw her eye was bright,
A well of love, a spring of light.

But now her looks are coy and cold,
  To mine they ne'er reply,
And yet I cease not to behold
  The love-light in her eye:
Her very frowns are fairer far,
Than smiles of other maidens are.

CLXXX.

THOMAS HOOD,
1798—1845.

THE DEATH-BED.

WE watched her breathing through the night,
 Her breathing soft and low,
As in her breast the wave of life
 Kept heaving to and fro.

So silently we seemed to speak,
 So slowly moved about,
As we had lent her half our powers
 To eke her living out.

Our very hopes belied our fears,
 Our fears our hopes belied—
We thought her dying when she slept,
 And sleeping when she died.

For when the morn came dim and sad,
 And chill with early showers,
Her quiet eyelids closed—she had
 Another morn than ours.

CLXXXI.

FAIR INES.

O SAW ye not fair Ines?
　　She's gone into the west,
To dazzle when the sun is down,
And rob the world of rest:
She took our daylight with her,
The smiles that we love best,
With morning blushes on her cheek,
And pearls upon her breast.

O turn again, fair Ines,
Before the fall of night,
For fear the moon should shine alone,
And stars unrivalled bright ;
And blessed will the lover be
That walks beneath their light,
And breathes the love against thy cheek
I dare not even write !

Would I had been, fair Ines,
That gallant cavalier,
Who rode so gaily by thy side,
And whispered thee so near !

Were there no bonny dames at home,
Or no true lovers here,
That he should cross the seas to win
The dearest of the dear ?

I saw thee, lovely Ines,
Descend along the shore,
With bands of noble gentlemen,
And banners waved before ;
And gentle youth and maidens gay,
And snowy plumes they wore ;—
It would have been a beauteous dream,
—If it had been no more !

Alas, alas ! fair Ines,
She went away with song,
With Music waiting on her steps,
And shoutings of the throng ;
But some were sad and felt no mirth,
But only Music's wrong,
In sounds that sang ' Farewell, farewell,
To her you've loved so long.'

Farewell, farewell, fair Ines,
That vessel never bore
So fair a lady on its deck,
Nor danced so light before,—

Alas ! for pleasure on the sea,
And sorrow on .the shore ;
The smile that blest one lover's heart
Has broken many more !

WINTHROP MACKWORTH PRAED,
1802—1839.

CLXXXII.

TIME'S SONG.

O'ER the level plains, where mountains greet me as I
    go,
O'er the desert waste, where fountains at my bidding flow,
On the boundless beam by day, on the cloud by night,
I am riding hence away: who will chain my flight?

War his weary watch was keeping,—I have crushed his
    spear ;
Grief within her bower was weeping,—I have dried her
    tear ;
Pleasure caught a minute's hold,—then I hurried by,
Leaving all her banquet cold, and her goblet dry.

Power had won a throne of glory : where is now his fame?
Genius said 'I live in story :' who hath heard his name?
Love beneath a myrtle bough whispered ' Why so fast?'
And the roses on his brow withered as I past.

19

I have heard the heifer lowing o'er the wild wave's bed ;
I have seen the billow flowing where the cattle fed ;
Where began my wanderings? Memory will not say !
Where will rest my weary wings ? Science turns away !

CLXXXIII.

FUIMUS !

GO to the once loved bowers ;
   Wreathe blushing roses for the lady's hair :
     Winter has been upon the leaves and flowers,—
       They were !

   Look for the domes of kings ;
Lo ! the owl's fortress, or the tiger's lair ;
     Oblivion sits beside them ; mockery sings
       They were !

   Waken the minstrel's lute ;
Bid the smooth pleader charm the listening air :
     The chords are broken, and the lips are mute ;—
       They were !

   Visit the great and brave ;
Worship the witcheries of the bright and fair.
     Is not thy foot upon a new-made grave ?—
       They were !

Speak to thine own heart ; prove
The secrets of thy nature.   What is there?
  Wild hopes, warm fancies, fervent faith, fond love,—
    They were !

  We too, we too must fall ;
A few brief years to labour and to bear ;—
  Then comes the sexton, and the old trite tale,
    ' We were ! '

CLXXXIV.   THOMAS LOVELL BEDDOES,
                            1803—1849.

WOLFRAM'S DIRGE.

I F thou wilt ease thine heart
   Of love and all its smart,
      Then sleep, dear, sleep;
And not a sorrow
   Hang any tear on your eyelashes;
      Lie still and deep,
   Sad soul, until the sea-wave washes
The rim o' the sun to-morrow,
   In eastern sky.

But wilt thou cure thine heart
Of love and all its smart,
      Then die, dear, die;
'Tis deeper, sweeter,
   Than on a rose bank to lie dreaming
      With folded eye;
   And then alone, amid the beaming
Of love's stars, thou'lt meet her
      In eastern sky.

CLXXXV.

SONG.

A HO! A ho!
Love's horn doth blow,
And he will out a-hawking go.
His shafts are light as beauty's sighs,
And bright as midnight's brightest eyes,
  And round his starry way
The swan-winged horses of the skies,
With summer's music in their manes,
Curve their fair necks to zephyr's reins,
  And urge their graceful play.

  A ho! A ho!
 Love's horn doth blow,
  And he will out a-hawking go.
The sparrows flutter round his wrist,
The feathery thieves that Venus kissed
  And taught their morning song,
The linnets seek the airy list,
And swallows too, small pets of spring,
Beat back the gale with swifter wing,
  And dart and wheel along.

A ho ! A ho !
Love's horn doth blow,
And he will out a-hawking go.
Now woe to every gnat that skips
To filch the fruit of ladies' lips,
        His felon blood is shed ;
And woe to flies, whose airy ships
On beauty cast their anchoring bite,
And bandit wasp, that naughty wight,
        Whose sting is slaughter-red.

NOTES.

NOTES.

IV. *The Paradise of Dainty Devices*, in which this poem first appeared, was published in 1576. It is said to have been 'devised and written' for the most part by *M.*—Mr.—*Edwards*, sometime Master of the Singing-boys at the Chapel Royal. But if this be so, the book did not see the light till at the least six, and probably ten, years after his death.

V. In *The Paradise of Dainty Devices*, 1576, this poem is given to *Richard Hunnis*, sometime Master of the Singing-boys at the Chapel Royal. Even as ascribed to him, it varies considerably in different editions, but it also appears with great divergences among the poems attributed to *Wyatt* in *Tottel's Miscellany*, 1557. In *Windet's* edition of *Songs and Sonnets, written by the Right Hon. Henry Howard, Earl of Surrey and Others*, 1585, in which also the poem is printed, the words 'and others' allow us to infer that *Tottel* may have been in error in regard to the authorship.

XII. This poem first appears in *The Phœnix
Nest*, 1593, signed neither with name nor initials, and
though usually ascribed to, may not with certainty be
declared to be by *Raleigh.*

XIII. *Dispraise of Love* was first printed anony-
mously in *The Poetical Rhapsody*, 1602, and is usually
ascribed to *Raleigh.*

XIV. These lines are quoted by *George Puttenham*
in his *Art of English Poesy*, 1589, as an instance of
'*Epimone*, or the Love burden.' In the Section 'Of
Ornament,' Lib. iii, he thus speaks : ' The Greek Poets
who made musical ditties to be sung to the lute or
harp, did use to link their staves together with one
verse running throughout the whole song by equal
distance, and was, for the most part, the first verse of
the staff, which kept so good sense and conformity
with the whole, as his `often repetition did give it
greater grace. They called such linking verse *Epimone*, the Latins *versus intercalaris*, and we may term
him the Love-burden, following the original, or, if it
please you, the long repeat : in one respect because
that one verse alone beareth the whole burden of the
song according to the original : in another respect for
that it comes by large distances to be often repeated,
as in this ditty made by the noble knight *Sir Philip
Sidney* " *My true love hath my heart, and I have his.*"'

In the *Arcadia,* however, 1598, it appears as a sonnet by the omission of the refrain as here, and the addition of six lines, the final one being the refrain.

XXII.   From *Greene's Pastoral Romance, Mena-phon.*   ' What manner of woman is she, quoth Meli-certus? As well as I can, answered Doron, I will make description of her :

Like to Diana, &c.

Thou hast, quoth Melicertus, made such a description as if Priamus' young boy should paint out the perfection of his Greekish paramour.'

XXIII.   From *Pandosto, or The Triumph of Time,* 1588, called in some later editions *Dorastus and Fawnia,* the prose romance of *Greene,* on which *Shakspere* founded his *Winter's Tale.* The lines are written by Dorastus in praise of Fawnia, the characters of which correspond to Florizel and Perdita.

XXV.   These lines are a paraphrase of a Greek Epigram, attributed by some to *Poseidippus,* by others to *Plato,* the Comic Poet, and by others to *Crates* the Cynic. The paraphrase is ascribed to *Bacon* by *Thomas Farnaby,* who published a collection of Greek Epigrams three years after *Bacon's* death, including the original epigram and the paraphrase, the only English lines in the book.

XXVI.   The Song of the First Chorus from *Hymen's Triumph, A Pastoral Tragi-comedy.*

XXVIII.   *England's Helicon*, 1600, is the authority for the ascription of this song to *Marlowe*, where however it appears in a different form to the version here quoted from the *Passionate Pilgrim*. The 'Answer' there given is probably by another hand. In *England's Helicon*, the 'Answer' consists of six stanzas, and bears the signature *Ignoto*, said to have been that often adopted by *Raleigh*.

XXIX.   No hint is found of the name of the author either in *England's Helicon*, 1600, or in *Byrd's Songs of Sundry Natures*, 1589, from which it was copied into *England's Helicon*.

XXX.   From *Much Ado About Nothing.*

XXXI.   From *A Midsummer Night's Dream.*

XXXII.   From *The Merchant of Venice*, 'whilst Bassanio comments on the caskets to himself.'

XXXIII.   From *The Tempest.*

XXXIV.   From *The Two Gentlemen of Verona.*

XXXV, XXXVI.   From *As You Like It.*

XXXVII, XXXVIII.   From *Twelfth Night, or What You Will.*

XXXIX. From *Henry VIII.*

Queen Katherine. *Take thy lute, wench: my soul grows sad*
with troubles;
Sing, and disperse 'em, if thou canst. Leave working.

XL, XLI. From *Cymbeline.*

XLIV. From *Patient Grissel, a Comedy, by Thomas Dekker, Henry Chettle, and William Haughton.* The song is almost universally attributed to *Dekker.*

XLV. From *The White Devil; or, Vittoria Corombona. Charles Lamb* in his *Specimens of English Dramatic Poets,* says 'I never saw anything like this dirge, except the ditty which reminds Ferdinand of his drowned father in *The Tempest.* As that is of the water, watery; so this is of the earth, earthy. Both have that intenseness of feeling which seems to resolve itself into the elements which it contemplates.'

XLVII. *Dr. Grosart* notices, in his edition of *Donne,* 1873, that the image of the compasses in this poem, used also elsewhere in the poet's works, 'was fetched from a family fact,' for the *Impressa* of *John Haywood, Donne's* maternal grandfather, was a compass with one foot in centre, the other broken, with the words '*Deest quod duceret orbam.*'

Ben Jonson, in his Verse Epistle to *Selden,* has the same image:

> *You have been*
> *Ever at home, yet have all countries seen ;*
> *And like a compass, keeping one foot still*
> *Upon your centre, do your circle fill*
> *Of general knowledge.*

L.   From *Cynthia's Revels*.

LI.   From *The Poetaster*.

LII.   From *The Silent Woman*.   The lines are imitated from the Latin verses of *Jean Bonnefons,* born 1554 at Clermont in Auvergne.   The poem makes a part of his *Pancharis,* in which he imitates *Catullus*.

LIII.   The boy thus renowned acted in *Cynthia's Revels* and in *The Poetaster*, in the years 1600 and 1601, in which year he probably died.

LIV.   From *Volpone ; or, The Fox*.   Imitated from *Catullus,*

> *Vivamus, mea Lesbia, atque amemus.*

LV.   Versified from passages in letters of *Philostratus the Sophist*.

LVII.   From *A Celebration of Charis, in Ten Lyric Pieces*.   The last two stanzas are given also in *The Devil is an Ass* as a song of Wittipol.

LVIII.   *Jonson* did not always admire the King's new cellar built by Inigo Jones.   He laughs at 'The cave for wine or ale' in the lines to *Inigo Marquis Would-Be*.   The dedication was written when the match with the Infanta was in contemplation, and Charles was at the Spanish court. Charles embarked on Feb. 14th, 1623.

LXI. From *The Rape of Lucrece.* It is also printed among the *Epithalamions* in *Heywood's Dialogues and Dramas.*

LXII. From *The Woman Hater.*

LXIII. From *The Faithful Shepherdess.*

LXIV. From *The Faithful Shepherdess.*

LXV. From *The Captain.*

LXVI. From *Valentinian.*

LXVII. From *The Nice Valour; or, The Passionate Madman.*

LXVIII. From *The Maid's Tragedy.*

LXIX. From *Blurt, Master Constable.*

XCII. From *Love in a Maze.*

XCIII. From *The Imposture.*

XCIV. From *The Contention of Ajax and Ulysses.* Sung before the body of Ajax, as going to the Temple.

XCIX. From *Comus*, which *Milton* himself called merely *A Masque presented at Ludlow Castle.*

C. From *Aglaura.*

CIII. *Anthony Wood* tells us that *Lucasta* was *Lucy Sacheverell*, 'a gentlewoman of great beauty and fortune, whom he usually called *Lux casta*, but she, upon a stray report that *Lovelace* was dead of his wound received at *Dunkirk*, soon after married.' This may reasonably be doubted, and *Lucasta* remains unknown.

CV. *Anthony Wood* tells us that after the pacification of *Berwick*, *Lovelace*, then a captain in the army, retired to his estate, Lovelace Place, near Canterbury. 'About which time he was made choice of by the whole body of the County of Kent to deliver the Kentish petition to the House of Commons for the restoring the King to his rights, &c. For which piece of service he was committed, April 30, 1642, to the Gatehouse at Westminster, where he made that celebrated song called *Stone walls do not a prison make, &c.*' *Althea*, like *Lucasta*, cannot be identified, but it is supposed that she became the poet's wife.

CXIII. From *The Mulberry Garden.*

CXV. The author and correct date are not known. The tune is earlier, being called 'new' in *The Crown Garland of Roses*, 1612. But the words are said to have first appeared in *Wit Restored*, 1658.

CXX. From *Acis and Galated.*

CXXI. This, a very early poem of *Pope*, is in part a paraphrase of *Horace's* Epode,

Beatus ille qui procul negotiis.

CXXII. An imitation of the lines of *Hadrian*,

Animula vagula blandula.

CXXIII. In the third edition of *Carey's Poems on Several Occasions,* MDCCXXIX, these verses first appear, prefaced by an 'Argument.' In this, after having denied the 'vulgar error' of those who imagined *Sally Salisbury* their subject, he says: 'The real occasion was this: A shoemaker's prentice making holiday with his sweetheart, treated her with a sight of *Bedlam*, the *Puppet-shows*, the *Flying-chairs*, and all the elegancies of *Moorfields*. From whence proceeding to the *Farthing Pie-house*, he gave her a collation of buns, cheese-cakes, gammon of bacon, stuffed beef and bottled ale ; through all which scenes the author dodged them, charmed with the simplicity of their courtship, from whence he drew this little sketch of nature. But being then young and obscure, he was very much ridiculed by some of his acquaintance for this performance, which nevertheless made its way into the polite world, and amply recompensed him by the applause of the divine *Addison*, who was

20

pleased more than once to mention it with approba-
tion.'

CXXIV. *Robert Levett,* who died Jan. 16th, 1782,
aged about seventy-eight, an Englishman by birth, had
been waiter in a coffee-house in Paris, where he
attracted the notice of some surgeons who frequented
it.   They subscribed to give him a surgical training.
He lived for twenty years with *Johnson,* who never
allowed him to be treated as a dependant.

CXXV.   Written in commemoration of the English
who fell in the battle of Culloden, April 16th, 1746.

CXXVI. Designed to be introduced into *Shakspere's Cymbeline.*

CXXVII.   From *The Vicar of Wakefield.*

CXXVIII.   Addressed to *Mrs. Unwin* in the
autumn of 1798.

CXXX.   From *The Seraglio,* where it is called *A
Rondeau.*

CXLI.   *Miss Wordsworth* in *Recollections of a Tour
made in Scotland,* A.D. 1803, says : ' It was harvest
time, and the fields were quietly—might I be allowed
to say pensively—enlivened by small companies of
reapers.   It is not uncommon in the more lonely parts
of the Highlands to see a single person so employed.

The following poem—" Behold her single in the field "
—was suggested to *William* by a beautiful sentence in
Thomas Wilkinson's Tour in Scotland.' On this
Mr. Shairp notes 'Probably one of *Wilkinson's*
poems of which *Wordsworth* speaks occasionally in
his letters.'

CXLII. From *Marmion.*

CXLIII. From *Rokeby.* Sir *Walter Scott* says of
this : ' The last verse is taken from the fragment of an
old Scottish ballad, of which I recollected only two
verses when the first edition of *Rokeby* was published.'
The original verse, the third of five, is :

> *He turned him round and right about,*
> *All on the Irish shore ;*
> *He gave his bridle-reins a shake,*
> *With, Adieu for evermore,*
> *My dear !*
> *Adieu for evermore !*

CXLIV. From *The Bride of Lammermoor.*

CXLV. From *Quentin Durward.*

CXLVI. From *The Doom of Devorgoil.* This is
an earlier version of the last song. Sir *Walter Scott*
says in his notes to *The Doom of Devorgoil,* ' The
author thought of omitting this song, which was in
fact abridged into one in *Quentin Durward,* termed
County Guy.'

CXLVII.   The three last lines were quoted by *Sir Walter Scott* in *Ivanhoe*, 1820, while the fragment was still unpublished, as follows : 'To borrow lines from a contemporary poet who has written too little,

> *The knights are dust,*
> *And their good swords are rust ;*
> *Their souls are with the saints we trust.*'

This convinced *Coleridge* that *Scott* wrote the novel, for the lines had been composed as an experiment in metre, and recited by *Coleridge* to a friend, who repeated them to *Scott* at a dinner-party, next day.

CXLVIII.   The poem ends as here in its early versions in *The Bijou*, 1828, and in the *Literary Souvenir* of the same date.   Some lines which now are often tacked on to it were published in *Blackwood's Magazine* for June, 1832, under the title *The Old Man's Sigh, a Sonnet*.   The lines are not a sonnet, and are of very inferior merit to the original poem.

CXLIX.   From *Zapolya, Part II, or The Usurper's Fate*.

CLI.   *Hester* was *Hester Savory*, of whom *Lamb* writes to *Manning* in 1803, 'I send you some verses I have made on the death of a young Quaker you may have heard me speak of as being in love with for some years while I lived at Pentonville, though I had never spoken to her in my life. She died about a month since.'

CLIV.   The battle of Hohenlinden was fought on December 3rd, 1800.

CLVIII.   From *Maid Marian.*

CLIX.   From *The Misfortunes of Elphin.*

CLX.   From *Crotchet Castle.*

CLXI.   From *Crotchet Castle.*

CLXII.   From *Gryll Grange.*

CLXIII.   Written by *Lord Byron* in 1815, on returning from a ball-room, where he had seen *Mrs. Wilmot Horton*, in mourning, with numerous spangles on her dress.

CLXVIII.   These lines were written for the Irish air *Gramachree,* but *Wolfe* denied that 'he had any real incident in view or had witnessed any immediate occurrence which might have prompted them.'

CLXIX.   At *Corunna,* Jan. 16th, 1809.

CLXXXIV.   From *Death's Jest-Book, or The Fool's Tragedy.*

CLXXXV.   From *The Bride's Tragedy.*

INDEX OF FIRST LINES.

INDEX OF FIRST LINES.

www.ingramcontent.com/pod-product-compliance
Lightning Source LLC
Chambersburg PA
CBHW031030120726
47905CB00007B/2127